AN UNBALANCED FORCE

AN UNBALANCED FORCE

VALERIE SHERRARD

We acknowledge financial support for our publishing activities: the Government of Canada, through the Canada Book Fund and The Canada Council for the Arts; the Government of Ontario, through the Ontario Arts Council, Ontario Creates, and the Ontario Book Publishing Tax Credit.

Library and Archives Canada Cataloguing in Publication

Title: An unbalanced force / Valerie Sherrard.
Names: Sherrard, Valerie, author.
Identifiers: Canadiana (print) 2024036130X | Canadiana (ebook) 20240361318 | ISBN 9781770867642 (softcover) | ISBN 9781770867659 (EPUB)
Subjects: LCGFT: Detective and mystery fiction. | LCGFT: Novels.
Classification: LCC PS8587.H3867 U53 2024 | DDC jC813/.6—dc23

United States Library of Congress Control Number: 2024934028

Cover and interior text design: Marijke Friesen
Manufactured by Friesens in Altona, Manitoba in September, 2024.

Printed using paper from a responsible and sustainable resource, including a mix of virgin fibres and recycled materials.

Printed and bound in Canada.

DCB Young Readers
An imprint of Cormorant Books Inc.
260 Ishpadinaa (Spadina) Avenue, Suite 502, Tkaronto (Toronto), ON
M5T 2E4, Canada

Suite 110, 7068 Portal Way, Ferndale, WA 98248, USA

www.dcbyoungreaders.com
www.cormorantbooks.com

For Albert
with much love

An object at rest remains at rest

and

an object in motion remains in motion

at the same speed and in the same direction

unless

acted upon by an unbalanced force.

Isaac Newton's First Law of Motion

TEN YEARS AGO
CHAPTER ONE

When I was seven years old, my father saved me from certain death.

That is a truth that lives in me. It forms itself into the shapes and colors of my world, and rises with me every morning, as faithful as the sun.

I am here today, and not reduced to what is politely referred to as "remains," because of my dad.

For a number of years after that day, I had a great need to hear the details of my rescue again and again. Often, I coaxed the story from my mother while she cooked dinner or folded clothes or when the two of us were running errands in the car.

There was something about hearing it told to me — something about the story itself — that seemed strangely solid, as though it was a trophy I could display on a shelf. How or why those words formed themselves into a kind of possession I can't explain. They just did.

"You had just turned seven," my mother would begin. And then, without fail, she would pause.

I always wondered what those pauses meant. It may be that she was giving me time to transport myself to that day in memory.

Or perhaps those few seconds were for her — a chance to steel herself against the emotions she was about to relive.

"We were living in the south end of the city," she would say when she was ready to continue. "You remember the place, Ethan — the beige two-story house with white shutters at the windows. Your room was blue with beautiful white clouds painted around the top of the walls. The previous tenants left it that way and you never wanted us to change it."

I have vivid memories of those clouds. As night fell, they seemed to swell and billow in the dancing shadows cast by a nearby streetlight. They weren't part of the story, but Mom had her own way of telling it, and I never tried to hurry her.

"You weren't supposed to leave the yard by yourself. Not ever."

Sometimes Mom would look at me then. Look right into my eyes, as if she needed to reassure herself that I was actually there, that my disobedience hadn't stolen me from her. Other times, she'd hurry on to the next part.

"And of all the places you could have wandered off to, you decided to make your way to the only empty house on the block."

That big old empty house was like a seven-year-old-boy magnet. I'd discovered the place not long after we'd moved to that neighborhood and had already been there more times than I could remember.

"I don't know what possessed you to do such a thing, but you actually went into the house!"

Reproach has crept into her voice at this point in the story and I'm not one hundred percent sure it's all for me. Has Mom really never considered that I had probably been on the vacated property lots of other times?

Maybe not. To get there, she'd have to admit she was a stay-at-home mother who often had no idea where her kid was.

And then she'd tell the rest of the story — as she knew it. Mom's account was soft and gentle, free of the terror of that afternoon. I wrapped her version around mine like a bandage.

But partial truths will not do today.

The empty house was faded brick, a tired-looking place. In the heat of the summer, it had a stillness that other homes — homes that are lived in — did not. That stillness gave it an air of mystery. It summoned me with its breathless, heavy silence.

It drew me in.

The windows on the lower levels were loosely boarded up, with spiderwebs and bits of leaves and such in between the wooden slats that had been hammered in place. Whoever had nailed the boards on hadn't taken many pains at the job. Otherwise, it's doubtful the fingers of a seven-year-old boy could have pried off the single slat of wood that half-heartedly covered a small basement window at the back of the house.

Brushing aside the detritus, I pushed my face close to the pane of glass and squinted through the film of grime that covered it. Except for a hulking shape I later discovered was the furnace, the basement was nothing more than a dark haze from where I squatted.

Oh, but it promised more if I could get myself onto the other side of that pane of glass.

The window was an old aluminum slider, seized up with dirt and inactivity. It moved an inch or two in response to my tugs and then refused to budge any further. I pulled and strained to no avail and was close to giving up a few times but the prize of getting into the house kept me going.

And then, quite to my surprise, the window yielded with a sideways jerk. Seconds later, with my heart nearly bursting, I had dropped to the floor inside and was tiptoeing through the deep gray shadows. The air smelled like dirty socks and swamp water and something sharp I couldn't identify.

A quick scan of the room told me there was nothing worth exploring down there so I made my way up to the main floor, relieved to find the door at the top of the steps unlocked. There wasn't much more on that level than there'd been downstairs — an old sideboard and a tall child's chair with foldout steps, which saved the day when I was ready to leave and found I needed something to climb on to reach the window I'd come in. The final object downstairs was a cracked mirror leaning against a wall in an open hallway closet.

I went from room to room. I walked around the perimeter of each one. As I moved about, a peculiar feeling grew in me, which I can only describe as a sense of ownership. This feeling gained strength and seemed more real with each subsequent visit. I reveled in the thrill that I was alone, and no one knew where I was.

I was in *my* house.

On the day of the incident — which happened after at least half a dozen visits there — I discovered the purpose of a pole that had been left in an upstairs bedroom closet. It was a plain wooden pole except for a metal hook on one end and I'd taken to carrying it with me, sometimes thumping it on the floor as I walked around, other times brandishing it like a sword.

On this particular foray, I'd been exploring upstairs when I noticed, for the first time, a framed rectangle on the ceiling of the second-floor hallway. I knew it had to be a passage to the attic and quickly realized the pole was the key to opening it. I fetched it and spent the next few minutes poking the pole's hook at a metal loop until, suddenly, it took hold and a drop-down ladder descended.

For several seconds I could do nothing but stand and stare, trying to take in the incredible luck of finding a way to expand my explorations.

Then I climbed up and into the attic. There wasn't the slightest chance that I could have done anything else.

I can say with certainty that the attic would have become my favorite part of the house ... if that day had turned out differently.

It was a wonderful space, with a floor that stretched the full length and width of the building. Two walls slanted and met at the top, so I knew they were the insides of the roof — made up of boards held in place by heavy wooden rafters. The end walls, which were triangular, each boasted a small rectangular window, topped by a framed dome of glass.

I hurried across the floor to the closest window, passing by various items that were strewn about. Some of them begged exploration but everything else could wait, would have to wait, having been pushed aside by my immediate desire to look out over the neighborhood.

To see without being seen.

The thought filled me with a peculiar sense of power.

But the glass on the window was murky, covered with a greasy film of grime. I rubbed at a spot with the back of my fist but all it did was smear the dirt. If I was to see the world below, I would need to open the window.

This one proved even more difficult than the stubborn basement window through which I'd first gained entry. I pushed and pulled, tugged and strained without budging it even a tiny sliver.

Eventually, I realized that this window was not merely stuck — it was sealed around the edges with paint.

I remembered my mother complaining that the windows had been painted shut in the apartment we'd occupied before moving to this neighborhood. She'd banged on them with her open palm and ruined one of her paring knives carving along the joints. Finally, she'd loosened them enough to open.

I had no knife, which left me with the solitary hope that banging on them would be enough to do the trick. Working my way around the frame, I smacked my palm on it just as Mom had done, pausing now and then to test the window. After several rounds of this, I convinced myself it was starting to give and doubled my efforts. I made a fist and hit harder, pounding with all the fury of my determination.

Until, that is, I missed the frame and smashed my fist into the glass — smashed it *through* the glass, actually. The sickening realization of what I'd done came over me slowly. I stood frozen in place, my small arm thrust through a jagged hole of shards. Several filthy glass spears were embedded in my flesh. There was a deep gash that clearly spelled trouble. Blood was gushing from it at an alarming rate, and I knew I needed to get help as quickly as possible.

Even so, it probably took me a full minute before I got up the courage to pull my arm back through. As careful as I tried to be, it was impossible to avoid adding more cuts to my trembling limb. The shards still clung to me as well, and I pulled them out unsteadily with my other hand.

My knees had begun to quake by the time I crossed the floor to the ladder and started to climb down. As I descended, clutching the rungs hands-over-head, blood ran across my armpit and began to soak my T-shirt. It was brand new, and the thought skittered through my brain that Mom wasn't going to be happy when she saw it.

The total blood loss couldn't have been great at that point, even though it looked like an enormous amount to me, so I have to assume my next movements were dictated by the confusion of fear.

Instead of getting out of the house and running straight home, I found myself standing in the upstairs hallway, staring at the opening in the ceiling. Tears filled my eyes and spilled over at the realization that I'd left the stick up there, and therefore had no way to close the door to the attic. Not for a single second did it occur to me that I could leave it there, leave the door open and the ladder down. In the panic of the moment, I was gripped by the need to cover my tracks.

It took everything in me to keep from bawling as I made my way back into the attic, retrieved the stick and climbed down for the second time. That was when I discovered I lacked the strength to hoist the heavy wooden ladder back into place. I shoved and shoved but could do no more than raise it halfway before my young arms began to tremble from the effort. After several attempts, it finally came to me that my energy would be better spent in getting home.

By the time I made my way to the first floor and then to the basement, I was feeling woozy. Blood loss and shock were taking their toll and as I climbed up to the window and leaned forward to crawl through it, the chair I was using tipped sideways and went crashing to the concrete floor below. It left me half in and half out, draped over the sill and unable to get a purchase inside or out.

Despair came over me, but it was tempered by a kind of exhaustion I'd never experienced before. It actually occurred to me that I could bleed to death, that indeed, I could die, but this thought came with an odd feeling of indifference.

It's there that my own memory blurs and fades to black. Luckily, Mom's version of events is there to fill in the gaps.

"It was the strangest thing, your father stopping by that afternoon. Said he just happened to be nearby — on the way to an appointment — but he'd never done that before."

My Grandma Martel had her own views. "Divine intervention," she whispered from her hospice bed. "The Good Lord sent him to save you, Ethan. Never doubt it."

Mom winked at me and gave Grandma a smile as if she was humoring a small child. I didn't like that. For all she knew, Grandma could be right.

"I don't know what distracted me from watching you that day," Mom would continue. "I was frantic when your father told me you weren't in the yard. We both called and called, and then he said he was going to circle the block."

Dad's search of the block was the next part of her story. A strange compulsion that drew him into the backyard of the abandoned house where he found me, bleeding and unconscious, halfway out of the basement window.

I must have surfaced for a moment as he lifted me out, for there's a vague and hazy memory of him fastening his necktie around my arm to stop the bleeding, his ashen face close to mine, and words tumbling through the years in my memory.

"Hold on, son. Hold on." And then, "Please, God. Please, please —"

I slipped back into the darkness after that and remember nothing else until the hospital. Which is where Mom's story wraps up.

"The doctor said another half hour and you'd have been gone."

Always *gone*, never *dead*. I don't think she could make herself say anything quite so final.

I was in the hospital long enough to be bored of the place and longing for better food. (At seven, that basically meant pizza and burgers.) By the time I got back home, the abandoned house had been closed up with heavy plywood, held in place with an abundance of screws.

I never got in there again.

It was only a month or two later that my grandma died, and Mom inherited the family home. We moved into it in short order.

That was the start of changes I could never have predicted.

PRESENT DAY
CHAPTER TWO

There's a reason for every lie.

Most of the time you don't have to look very hard to find that reason. But now and then you come across a lie you just cannot explain. One that shoves all the other things in your head into a corner and jabs at your gut until you feel like you've been kicked good and hard.

I was thinking about that as I sat under a tree by a brook that runs into the Gatineau River — my go-to place when I need to sort things out. I'd been there plenty of times before, but the details of earlier visits have faded. This one is crystal clear in my memory.

It was a Saturday and the last day of June. Actually, the last day of a lot of things.

I'd spent the morning itching to get outside and onto my new Trek trail bike, which had been a complete surprise.

"Thought you might like an upgrade to get you ready for the Inca Trail," Dad had told me after supper the previous day.

I turned to see him wheeling the bike into our media room where I was browsing on-demand selections.

Mom was on the couch, waiting to veto or approve my choice for movie night. She frowned.

"I don't think that's actually been settled," she said without looking up.

"Yes, well, just in case you *do* get to go." Dad gave me a wink.

I checked out the bike, sidestepping the subject of whether or not the trip to Peru was going to happen. I'd been salivating over the thought of doing the Inca Trail for more than a year, ever since Mom coaxed me into watching a documentary about Machu Picchu with her. It's pretty amazing and I'd spent a fair amount of time exploring it online. My interest in the place had turned into a deal.

There are a lot of deals in our house. This one had been about my grades in language arts, and I might as well admit I'd been coasting a lot this year. I find it hard to get into someone else's idea of a good story. I'm not a big reader and when I do pick up a book, I want it to be something that's interesting to me.

So, the folks had come up with the idea of the Inca Trail as a reward for shaping up. I'd made an effort, for a while anyway, but the results hadn't been spectacular. To be honest, since we wouldn't be going until the winter break in the coming school year, I figured there was still plenty of time. I knew Mom wouldn't think I'd done enough, but that didn't mean Dad couldn't talk her into it.

Meanwhile, there was a new bike to break in. Which honestly had nothing to do with Peru — we'll have rental bikes there, if we do end up going.

The Trek was a beauty and my first thought this morning was about hitting some trails but a glance out the window vetoed that idea. The sky was heavy with dark clouds, from which a steady drizzle was falling. I'd grabbed my phone to see if the rain was going to last all day when there was a tap on my door.

"You up, Ethan?"

"Yeah, Dad. Come on in."

"They're calling for sun later this morning," he said, motioning toward the rainfall outside the window. Sometimes it's like he can read my mind. "I know you're probably anxious to get on that new bike."

"Definitely."

"Anyway, I'm just heading to the airport. Thought I'd leave you a few bucks, in case you need anything."

Need wasn't quite the right word. I never *need* anything, not since Dad hit the big time with his business. My girlfriend, Nora, would be quick to point out that people in "my world" know nothing about need (or a whole lot of other things). You'd think she came from a slum, the way she goes on about the haves and have-nots — an attitude she gets from her mom, who's always griping about the things they don't have. Truth is, her family lives just a few blocks away from the gated Ottawa community I call home.

I had a twinge of guilt at the thought of taking the pair of fifties Dad was holding out. I haven't even touched my allowance this week and there's a metal box in the bottom of my closet that's half full of money I've stashed over the years.

I told him, "I'm good, Dad," but he thrust the bills into my hand anyway.

"You never know what might come up."

"Okay. Well, thanks."

"You bet." He looked happy. "Anyway, gotta run. My flight is at eleven."

He gave me a pat on the shoulder then, and disappeared out the door. Not a word of caution to not tell Mom about the cash — he knows that's not necessary. Some rules write themselves as you go along.

Downstairs, Mom was sitting at the kitchen island, nibbling a wedge of cantaloupe. Steam rose from a cup of black coffee in front of her, so I knew she hadn't been up for long.

"Your father just left for his business trip," she said.

"Yeah. He stopped by my room to say goodbye." I dumped milk, whey protein isolate, and frozen raspberries into the blender.

Mom gave my breakfast an approving glance as she reached for a cup of low-fat yogurt and spooned some granola on top.

"Any plans for the day? When is Owen back?"

"Not until Monday," I said, and though she hadn't asked, I added, "and Nora's working."

Mom didn't quite manage to hide a frown at the mention of Nora's name. My folks liked her a lot when we first started dating. In fact, they liked her so much they even invited her mom and dad over for barbecues a couple of times. But that all changed when they saw the "on again off again" way our relationship has gone.

At the moment it's "on" and Nora refuses to understand why they aren't as friendly as they used to be.

The guy Mom asked about — Owen Cass — is my closest friend, and he's been a *lot* more vocal about Nora than my parents. He razzes me about her on a pretty regular basis with comments like, "Ever think about getting a girlfriend who doesn't enjoy torturing you?"

She doesn't really. Torture me, that is. Sure, she can be unpredictable, and yes, sometimes her reactions seem kind of over-the-top, but I can handle that. It's when she won't speak to me for days and I have *no clue why* — that's the one thing I really hate. I've even thought about making a clean break a couple of times when that's happened, but when she came around, I always just let it go. I could probably never explain why to Owen or my folks or anyone, including me. Something about her makes me willing to wait out the tough times.

Her absolutely authentic laugh, for example, and the way she tilts her head back and lets it burst out. Or how she leans against my shoulder and looks up with her eyes all serious and intense, and says, "I'm so happy," when things are good.

Owen says I could do better. My folks don't say much of anything. They mostly let their disapproval come through in the things they don't say. Like that moment at breakfast when Mom moved past the way I mentioned her just as if she hadn't heard.

"Well, don't spend all day in front of the computer."

"I'm going to try out the new bike later if it clears up." I picked up my protein shake and went back to my room where I spent the next couple of hours playing video games. It wasn't until lunch, when Mom knocked and asked if I wanted to join her for a salad of baby spinach, pumpkin seeds, and tuna, that I realized the rain had stopped.

As soon as lunch was over, I headed out the door, slipping onto my new bike like it was an old friend. I've always loved bikes, the way they come to life under me, gliding along a street or bumping over a path.

This one is a beauty. It's light, but strong and solid and I trusted it immediately. I got the feel of it riding around the streets of the community before breaking out and heading south. I passed through the neighborhood where Nora lives, pulling into a gas station to pick up a bottle of water since I'd forgotten to bring my sports bottle with me.

After that I was off, riding seriously, letting the bike go wherever it wanted. An hour later I hit the outskirts of the city and circled back, taking my time because fatigue was starting to set in. The slower pace let me take in more details of my surroundings, or I might never have seen what I did a few moments later.

Three men in a strip mall parking lot, standing by a sleek black sedan. I didn't recognize the vehicle and I didn't recognize two of the men, but I knew the third.

It was my father.

I'd already gone past, but I stopped as soon as I could and pivoted to face them. It was too far to call out to him, so I sent a text, hoping to catch him before he got into the car.

Hi Dad

He reached into the pocket of his jacket, pulled out his phone, and swiped the screen. I watched as he tapped an answer, grinning to think how surprised he was going to be when I told him where I was.

My phone alerted me to his response.

Just off flight and getting into cab. Have to talk later.

I stared at the words, trying to make them make sense. Dad's plans sometimes change at the last minute, so the fact that he was still in the city hadn't seemed at all significant.

But the lie?

That I couldn't explain.

CHAPTER THREE

Time cannot stand still. I know that.

Even so, it *felt* as though everything had stopped. Or maybe it was me. Maybe I was standing still in time. Maybe the world kept ticking along and I wasn't moving forward with it. Like those people who get themselves cryogenically frozen with the hope they can get thawed out and have a new start someday.

The sedan had slid out of sight long before that feeling of being suspended lifted and I was able to turn my bike homeward and start pedaling again. I rode a few blocks on autopilot before realizing home was the last place I wanted to be right then.

Mom's not what you'd call a highly perceptive person but as shook up as I was feeling, even she would have noticed something was wrong. I had to assume I wasn't the only one my father was lying to. If that was right, and Mom was also in the dark about whatever he was up to, I figured it should probably stay that way, at least for the time being.

And after all, there could be a totally innocent explanation. Why risk upsetting Mom, maybe causing a big argument between her and Dad? Man, do I hate it when they fight. That can turn into days of tension and heavy silence.

Besides, I was already realizing I didn't want my father confronted about what I'd seen. Not by me *or* my mom. Because he'd have an explanation ready in a heartbeat, but there was basically zero chance anything he said would be the truth.

It's weird to admit that. My father lies a lot. He laughs about it and calls himself a smooth talker. I've heard him tell stories that I knew one hundred percent weren't true and I practically believed them myself. He'll describe the way he built the company that made us sort-of rich by starting in a low-level job and working his way through the ranks until he was in a position to buy the whole thing. Sounds great the way he tells it, except it's pure fantasy.

It was actually the inheritance from my grandmother that made it possible for him to set himself up in business. And sure, he's worked hard to make it a success, but he definitely didn't start at the bottom and climb to where he's at now.

I asked him one time, "Why the fiction?"

He threw his head back and laughed. Then he slapped my knee.

"That's the kind of savvy you *need* in the selling world, Ethan," he said. "A way to help clients feel connected and comfortable. Like you're one of them. Makes people want to do business with you."

His explanation didn't exactly help me understand why those lies were necessary, but it *did* get me noticing how often my father strayed from the truth.

Sometimes I knew because he'd give me a wink or a grin, like when he answered Mom's questions about how she looked: her hair, her clothes — that sort of thing. He gives a smooth compliment, my dad, never over-the-top, always including some specific detail. It was a bit troubling, the way his insincerity pleased her.

Other times, I could just tell he was lying. I learned to recognize a certain look in his eyes, when he didn't quite seem to be *present* in the conversation.

I suppose it had bothered me before now, but only a little bit. I'd never considered Dad's "storytelling" as any kind of big deal. Everyone lies sometimes, right? And there didn't seem to be any actual harm in the ones he was telling.

This was different. Different in a way that made my stomach hurt, almost like it did the first time Nora broke up with me. It was the kind of upset that messes with your whole system, throwing everything out of whack.

I needed to find out what was going on. If I had to confront my father at some point, I would, but not until I had some solid proof, something that would force him to tell me the truth.

A question popped up from the scramble of thoughts racing around in my head.

Proof of *what*?

My mouth was suddenly dry, and I stopped to gulp down a few swallows of water.

That was when it really hit me. Dad being away on business for days at a time has been a regular thing for years. But was it really? For all I knew, he could have been lying the entire time. Maybe he never leaves town at all.

Another question crept up my spine like cold fingers. If that turned out to be the case, then where had my father really been spending all those nights?

I'm not naive. Of course, it crossed my mind that he could be messing around on my mother. But that didn't fit the sedan and the men he'd been traveling with. My gut said that whatever was going on, it wasn't about a woman.

Unfortunately, that didn't help much. Ruling out one thing didn't clear up the mystery of what *was* going on. The lie, the unexplained absence — those questions were swirling around me like a dark fog.

While I sat there, straddling the bike, sipping water, and trying to steady my breathing, a text came in from Nora.

Hey! I got off shift early. ☺

I hadn't thought about whether or not I should tell any of this to Nora, but if I saw her now, she'd see that something was bothering me. There'd be questions, and lots of them.

Nope.

So, I just didn't answer her. I knew she'd try again one or two more times and then she'd get annoyed and make plans with one of her friends.

Meanwhile, I decided to head down to the Central Business District, where Dad has his office. It's one of those sleek, modern places where the firms are identified by discreet, high-end nameplates on the doors.

Dad's says, simply, The Granger Group. I'd tell you what the "group" does if I had an actual clue myself. I don't. Not that I haven't asked. I have, and was given a long explanation with a jumble of words from the world of finance, none of which I understood.

I wanted to, though. I even asked a few questions, like, "So, do you manage investments?" and, "Does your work involve stocks and stuff?"

Each of his answers started off with, "Not exactly, but —" and ended with me even more confused. So, no, I don't know what he does. I *do* know he makes a lot of money at it.

Nothing wrong with that, right? If a person works hard and gets ahead, then that's a good thing. I appreciate my dad putting in long hours so we can have a better life.

Except, there's a kind of uneasiness in me now. With what happened today, I have a lot of questions I never had before.

Going to his office might be a waste of time, but I needed to do *something* — to start digging for answers. Maybe I'd even find an innocent explanation for his pretending to be out of town. Dad is big on surprises — maybe he's working on something like that.

Whether or not I discovered anything, there was a kind of nervous energy humming in me. Going to Dad's workplace would at least give me something to do. First, though, I needed to swing by my house, drop off my bike, and get the spare key fob to his office. I knew I'd find that in the storeroom, which is on the same level as the garage. It's a large room used mainly for storage.

Aside from the stacks of boxes and a few items of furniture no longer in use, there's a space sectioned off in there where Dad has a kind of home workstation. He calls it his "storage office." A desk, a couple of swivel chairs, and a line of filing cabinets are arranged in the back corner near the room's only window. That's where he disappears to with his laptop when he's got work he can get done at home.

Ten minutes later, I wheeled my bike into the garage, parked it on a stand, and went down the hall that leads to the storeroom. For a few seconds I found myself looking at the door. It was like I'd never seen it before. Steel, with not one but two keypads that unlock dead bolts. I'm not the greatest at memorizing numbers, but Dad's system makes it easy. The bottom keypad is the only one I needed to remember, and those numbers, which would seem random to anyone else, had specific meaning to our family.

It was the date of that day so long ago, when my father saved my life.

The upper keypad used the same code except it started with the second number in the sequence and rotated back to the first one at the end.

As I punched in the codes to unlock the door, I realized I'd never questioned why that kind of security was needed in a room where, as far as I knew, nothing of any great value or importance was kept.

Except, as I'd just discovered, there were definitely things I *didn't* know. Whether or not they were of any great importance, well, that remained to be seen.

Maybe the office downtown was the wrong place to start exploring. There might be things in the storeroom that could answer some of my questions. So, for a couple of minutes, I poked around some of the boxes. They were all labeled but it would take time to see if the descriptions were accurate. And there were so many!

In the end, I opted to go ahead and stick with my original plan. Since it was Saturday, the office building wouldn't be busy. I should be able to go in, look around, and leave without being seen by too many people. The storeroom, I could take a look at any time.

The key fob was where I knew Dad kept it, hidden in a tall artificial plant that sat on the floor to the left of the desk. I tucked it securely into my pocket and ordered an Uber to pick me up on the corner of our street.

I might as well not have bothered. An hour after getting to the office I had to admit that I was wasting my time. Nothing I was able to access in the filing cabinets meant a thing to me. Files with pages and pages of charts, plus long sections with columns of figures — it might as well have been a foreign language. None of what I saw gave me the slightest hint as to whether it was legit, or to be honest, even *what* it was.

Being careful to leave everything just as it had been when I arrived, I let myself out, checked to be sure the door was secure, and headed for the lobby's main entrance.

Which is when I saw him. One of the men who'd been with my father earlier.

CHAPTER FOUR

Okay, I wasn't one hundred percent sure about that. I'd only glanced at the men with my father, so it could have been paranoia that made me think the guy standing by the information counter was one of them. There was just something about him, the way he looked so casual, the way I felt as if he was watching me without seeming to.

I panicked and made a beeline to the public men's room. As the door swung closed behind me, I realized that since the building was practically deserted, I was almost certain to be the only one in there, trapped with only one way out.

"All right, get a grip," I told myself. "Say that *is* one of the guys. What's he going to do? Come in here and rough me up? Why would he?"

It took a few minutes to convince myself the guy in the lobby probably wasn't one of the duo I'd seen earlier with my father, and that even if he was, his presence in the lobby couldn't possibly have anything to do with me.

All the same, I let a bit more time pass before I strolled casually (at least, that's what I was aiming for) back out there. The guy was nowhere to be seen.

I felt a bit foolish. Then I got mad. Whatever my dad was hiding, that was the cause of all the turmoil inside me. Even if there was a perfectly innocent explanation, which I doubted, his habit of lying made it impossible for me to just ask what was going on.

That was when I decided to head to my spot near the Gatineau. I needed to be alone, to figure out what to do, and to try to settle the churning in my gut. "My" place by the brook is just a few minutes' walk from where I had Uber driver number two drop me off and I could actually feel myself getting calmer as I neared it.

I don't know what it is about this spot, exactly. The sound of the stream gurgling toward the river, the way the air smells so clean, and the tucked-in feeling of being surrounded by trees and earth and water. It really helps me think more clearly — sitting back, taking long, deep breaths. It's almost as if my problems sort themselves out there.

The first thing that popped into my head was that the Uber drives I'd just taken were on my father's account. Why that hadn't occurred to me before I have no idea. If it had, I'd have grabbed a cab. Instead, I'd picked a mode of travel that was practically like leaving my dad a note saying I'd gone to his office. When he wasn't there.

How was I going to explain that if he asked? And I couldn't imagine a scenario where he'd realize I'd been there and not want to know why. Dad is a big fan of small details. It's his philosophy that if you know what's going on with the little things, the big things practically take care of themselves.

It was possible, but not likely, he'd never notice it. No, I needed to come up with some kind of cover story. In a twisted sort of way, it's almost unfortunate I didn't inherit my father's ability to lie in an effortless, believable way. I decided my best bet was to tell him something that was as close to the truth as possible.

Not the actual, exact truth of course. Telling him, "I was there doing a little snooping because I knew you weren't really out of town and I wanted to find out what else you might be hiding," didn't strike me as a winning approach. In case you were wondering.

By the way, I'm not big on lying. I don't think too many people are one hundred percent honest, and that's not what I'm claiming, but when I can, I prefer to tell the truth.

In this case, since complete honesty was obviously not going to work, I came up with a version that was kind of parallel to the truth.

And I made a mental note to be more careful about the trail I left. Taking Ubers had been such a dumb mistake I was practically embarrassed for myself.

Then I got mad again. The fact that I had to start covering my tracks felt foreign and kind of sleazy. It outraged me that my own father had put me in a position where I'd have to sneak and lie and snoop into who knows what. That I'd be in a paranoid enough state of mind to actually think there was something suspicious about a random stranger in a lobby of a building. And where I wouldn't feel like seeing Nora even though I had nothing else to do.

That reminded me — I still hadn't answered her message.

I pulled out my phone and shot off a quick text, feeling cruddy about the way I'd ignored her earlier. As I expected, there was no answer, but I suddenly really wanted to see her, so I tried again. Nothing.

The next thing I knew, I was waking up. It wasn't the first time I've fallen asleep in that spot. The way the shimmering water ripples can be hypnotic, but as upset as I'd been earlier, I wouldn't have predicted a nap.

I stretched and walked back out to the road. A glance at my phone told me it was nearly seven o'clock, which explained why I was hungry and thirsty. It also told me I'd slept through a text from Mom asking if I was going to be there for dinner. I sent a quick *sorry, on my way now* reply and started toward home.

When I got there a Post-it on the fridge reminded me Mom had gone to some artsy event. She's a huge fan of art of any kind and rarely misses a chance to attend exhibitions. Sometimes she buys a painting or sculpture or whatever too, but mostly she just enjoys mingling and talking to other people about whatever's on display. She dragged me along once, maybe hoping I'd prove to have the art-loving gene too. I don't. Not like her, anyway.

I checked inside the fridge — nothing of interest — and considered calling for delivery but decided I didn't want to wait. So, I ended up making a couple of grilled cheese sandwiches. Sent another text to Nora while I was eating. No answer.

I'd just stuck my plate and glass in the dishwasher when a memory hit me. Something from five, maybe six months ago. Mom and Dad having one of their quiet arguments — the kind that grab my interest. The raised voice squabbles I shut out. But the times when they obviously don't want to be heard, those get my attention.

This one had been about Dad's vehicle. I focused, trying to bring back the details. Dad had been out of town, but Mom had seen his SUV — or thought she had, pulling out of the parking lot of a critical care center, driven by a man she didn't recognize.

Dad had insisted she was wrong, that it was impossible since his car was parked at the airport the whole time. Said it wasn't the only car of that make on the road. And when Mom told him she'd seen the license plate and it was his, he persuaded her she'd misread it.

But I remember the way she kept looking at him for the next few days, like there was something simmering, mistrust or at least doubt. Even so, she didn't mention it again. Not that I know of anyway.

Thinking about it now, I recall how I had automatically — maybe instinctively — thought she probably *had* seen Dad's car. I'd figured he'd loaned it to someone while he was out of town and, for whatever reason, didn't want her to know. Or maybe he was just keeping his skills as a liar from getting rusty.

So, if Mom was right, and it was Dad's vehicle she'd seen, who'd been behind the wheel? And was my father really out of town that time?

If he habitually lied about being away on business, he'd be too smart to drive his own SUV around while he was supposed to be away. I knew for sure he was in the city now, but traveling in a vehicle that wasn't his.

These thoughts were interrupted as a horrifying idea hit me. Mom had seen Dad's SUV leaving the critical care center! Could it be that my dad was ill and hiding it from us? Had the man Mom saw been dropping him off for some kind of treatment? He hasn't *seemed* sick but that in itself doesn't prove much.

My head hurt. The more I thought about it, the more questions I had. And no solid ideas as to how I could find out the answers.

And then it hit me! Nora's mom works at that center.

CHAPTER FIVE

I didn't get a lot of sleep that night, but even so, by morning I thought I could manage a passable job of acting normal. A hot shower helped clear my head, after which I headed to the kitchen for breakfast.

Mom glanced up from her tablet when I crossed to the fridge. "Morning," she said. "So, how was the new bike?"

"Good," I said. It came out a bit strained, so I cleared my throat and added, "Great!"

My face warped into a guilty smile. Mom gave me a curious look, which told me I wasn't as convincing an actor as I thought I'd be. It was just my good luck then, when a ping from her tablet drew her attention back to whatever she'd been doing. Her turn on some kind of word game, most likely.

I devoured a muffin in a few large and not very well chewed bites, chugged a glass of orange juice, and got out of the house with a quick wave and "See you later."

Ignoring the Trek, I got on my old bike, stuck my water bottle in the holder, and took off, pedaling like someone was chasing me. Almost without realizing where I was headed, I found myself back at the place where I'd spotted my father the day before.

Whatever drove me there — whatever unconscious expectation nudged me to the scene of the crime, so to speak, all I found was an ordinary stretch along the road. Even so, I paused there, watching the buildings and vehicles and people, as if a clue was hidden somewhere in the humdrum of everyday routines.

I pulled out my phone and brought up yesterday's message from Dad. I was a lot calmer seeing it than I had been yesterday, but it still made my gut clench.

Just off flight and getting into cab. Have to talk later.

"You weren't, though," I said to no one. "You were standing right over there. You and your pals. Whoever they were."

Aside from registering their presence, I hadn't paid much attention to the men he'd been with, which almost made my reaction to the guy in the lobby yesterday amusing. I tried not to think about that and instead focused on the scene with my dad. Plus, the vague impression I'd formed of the guys he was with.

Both men were taller than my father, if I was remembering correctly. And they'd been dressed casually. Not jeans, but not suits either. One thing I was reasonably sure about — I'd never seen either of them before.

As I thought it through, it seemed probable they'd come from inside one of the stores in the background. Yet I was fairly certain no one had been carrying a bag, so they hadn't stopped to buy anything. And even if one of them had made a purchase, there'd have been no reason for all three of them to be out of the car.

I scanned the storefronts. There was nothing about any of them that stood out or offered the slightest hint. A pet food store, a leather repair shop, a bookstore, a floor cleaning company, and the usual convenience store.

Nothing helpful there. Not a single clue to say why he'd been at this particular place, or where they'd been heading when their sedan slid into traffic and sailed past the spot where I'd been standing.

Even so, I took pictures of each of the stores, just in case something tied in to one of them at some point. It seemed pretty lame, but since I'd found out exactly nothing so far, I realized I didn't know what might turn out to be important.

It didn't feel like much of an accomplishment.

With no other ideas to follow up, I shot off a text to Nora. She answered quickly and we agreed to meet at a juice bar she likes.

Her bike was there when I arrived. I secured mine next to it on the stand before heading inside. She saw me coming and lifted an arm to wave me over. Her other hand was busy spooning whipped cream into her mouth from the top of a mango smoothie — her favorite.

I slid into the seat across from her, determined to act one hundred percent normal. I thought I was doing great, but within a few minutes Nora's eyes narrowed.

"Are you breaking up with me?" she demanded.

"What? No!" I said.

"So, what's wrong then?"

I made myself meet her eyes, which stared back at me like penetrating lasers. It took everything I had not to look away.

"Nothing's wrong," I said.

Didn't help. After a moment, Nora shook her head.

"Oh yeah, *something's* wrong," she said. "Your face is weird."

"No, it's not," I said.

"If you're not going to tell me," she said, leaning closer, "I might as well go home."

"No, don't," I said. "And you're right. There *is* something bothering me."

"About *us*?"

"No." I reached over and took her hand, squeezing it lightly and giving her a reassuring smile. "Not at all."

"What then?"

"I don't want to talk about it here," I told her. True, but I was mostly buying time to sort out what to tell her.

Nora suggested we should go to a certain church cemetery. I can't say which one since the first time Nora took me there, I had to promise I'd never tell. That was because of a secret it held. Specifically, she'd buried her guinea pig, Barnaby, there. After he was dead, of course.

We sat near Barnaby's final resting place and Nora snuggled warmly against my chest, her face turned upward and the fingers of her right hand pressed flat over my heart.

"So?" she said. "What is it then?"

And right then, at that moment, it felt so safe, and *necessary* to let it all out. So, I made her promise (on Barnaby the guinea pig's memory) she wouldn't tell a soul, and I filled her in on yesterday's events.

By the time I'd finished she was sitting upright. It was hard to read her reaction because her expression kept changing. There was shock and disbelief but there were also hints of what looked a lot like excitement.

"I can't believe it!" she said when she'd heard the whole thing.

"Yeah. Me neither."

"So, what are you going to do?"

"What *can* I do?" I said. "I can't just ask him. Even if I did, he's not going to tell me the truth."

"How do you know?"

"Because he obviously has something to hide."

"You hear about people who have whole secret lives," Nora said. "Separate homes and families and everything."

"Right, except that idea doesn't fit what I saw," I said.

"Probably not," she agreed. But then she added, "Imagine if that *was* it though — you could even have half-siblings out there somewhere!"

"Yeah, I doubt that," I said. I could see she was warming to the secret family theory, and I didn't want to hear any more about it, so I added quickly, "There's one other thing that could be related."

She listened as I told her about Mom seeing Dad's vehicle at the care center, finishing with, "So, I guess there could be a health issue."

"My mother works there!" Nora said.

"Right," I said, as if I hadn't made that connection already. "What does she do, exactly?"

"Some kind of after-treatment support. But I think she'd have told me if she saw your dad there."

"Wouldn't that be confidential?"

"Yeah, I guess probably. She might have asked me something about him to see if I already knew, though. I don't remember her doing anything like that."

"It's a long shot, anyway," I said. "More than likely the guy who had Dad's vehicle that day just borrowed it for his own personal use."

"Probably," Nora agreed.

"Whatever's going on, I'd like to find a way to figure out what he's up to."

"You could follow him," Nora said.

"I don't think my bike can quite keep up," I said.

"Alana has a car," she said.

Alana is her nineteen-year-old sister, and it's true she has a car. It's also true the car is bright cobalt blue. Not exactly the kind of vehicle you want on a stealth mission. And that wasn't the only drawback.

"Your sister won't even give *you* a drive unless you pay her," I said. "I'd be better off hiring a private investigator."

Actually, paying wasn't the issue. I just didn't want to say her sister is about the last person I'd ever let in on something I didn't want spread all over the place. I don't think I've ever been in the same room with her that she wasn't gossiping about someone or other.

"Besides," I added, "I know I can trust you, but Alana, or really, anyone else who knew, might let something slip."

And that's where we left it. But an idea was starting to form.

CHAPTER SIX

The office building was squat and gloomy — a weary gray blot on the street — so it was a surprise to find myself in a bright, modern lobby when I entered. An information desk on the left was unstaffed but a directory next to the elevators told me where I needed to go.

The office of Abboud and Rayne was on the third floor, at the end of the hall stretching to my left. A slim sign on the door disclosed nothing about the type of investigative work offered by either Abboud or Rayne, but their website had promised discretion and satisfaction.

Inside, there was a small waiting area facing a vacant reception desk (did anyone actually work in this building?). I hesitated, sat for a moment, and was wondering how I should announce my presence when one of the two doors along the back wall opened, and a woman appeared.

She was clearly expecting to see someone, which told me there'd been some kind of alert when I entered. Just as obvious was the fact that she wasn't expecting *me*. Or rather, anyone of my age.

Even so, she crossed the space between us, smiling, and held her hand out. I stood and shook it as she introduced herself.

"Hello. I'm Imani Abboud, Private Investigator," she said.

"I'm Ethan Granger, student," I said. I don't know what made me put in the student part. I guess because she'd identified herself by name and occupation.

"What can I do for you, Ethan?" she asked.

I could tell she was sizing me up, looking for anything that might spell trouble. Checking to see if I was nervous. Or maybe high.

"I need an investigator," I said. "For a personal matter."

Ms. Abboud nodded. "I see," she said. "Come this way, please."

I followed her into the room she'd emerged from and took one of the chairs facing her desk. She seated herself and got right to the point.

"How old are you, Ethan?"

"Seventeen."

"I see. Well, I'm willing to hear you out, of course, but there are restrictions on the kind of contracts one can enter into with a minor."

"What kind of restrictions?"

"Essentially, the contract would have to benefit you in specific ways or provide you with a necessity of life."

"What would qualify as a necessity of life?" I asked.

"Food, clothing, medical care, housing, education — those are pretty much givens. Anything else depends on the circumstances."

"I think this might fit the 'anything else' part of that," I said.

"Okay then, I guess you'd better tell me why you're here," she said. "And I'll have to evaluate whether it would be ethical for me to help."

I told her about discovering my father's lie and how I wanted to know the truth. She listened without interrupting, except that she held a finger up as a signal for me to pause a couple of times when she wanted to write something on a yellow legal pad in front of her.

"I can pay," I said, when I'd told her everything I thought she needed to know. "I have some money saved up."

"Before we talk about that, *if* this meets the criteria as far as your age is concerned, I want to point out a few things," Ms. Abboud said. "It's entirely possible that there's an innocent explanation for your father's apparent duplicity."

That reminded me to mention his SUV being at the critical care center when he was supposed to be out of town. I gave her those details and said, "I don't know how that ties in, or even if it does."

Ms. Abboud nodded and made another note. Then she said, "The other thing is this — once you know something, you can't un-know it. It's important to realize that whatever you find out, it's going to be something you'll have to carry for the rest of your days."

She sat silently then as I let her words sink in.

"It feels like something I *have* to do," I said at last. "I mean, this is seriously messing with my head."

She nodded. "I understand this could be having a detrimental effect on you. In which case, I believe it narrowly meets the criteria."

"So you'll help me?"

"I'll certainly try. So, to begin, what's your father's name?"

"Stuart Granger."

She asked me his date of birth, some stuff about his routine, and how often he (she paused to do air quotes) "goes out of town."

"It's pretty much every week or two," I said. "But he always tells me ahead of time — usually the day before — when he's going to be away. And I usually know approximately what time he'll be leaving for the airport. Or wherever he's really going."

"That will be plenty of notice, and it will help keep your cost down," she told me. "A more general stakeout can add up pretty fast."

I was glad she'd finally mentioned money. I'd brought a thousand in cash and had almost two more in my stash at home, which I was hoping would be enough. There was also money in the bank if I needed more, but Mom is on that account, and I sure didn't want any questions from her.

"How much will the retainer be?" I asked.

"Let me get a standard contract first and then we'll discuss that," she said, tapping some keys on her laptop. I gave her details as she asked for them, and once she'd typed them in, she hit print and a machine atop a cabinet along the wall whirred to life.

Half an hour later, after Ms. Abboud had gone over the four pages that made up the contract, we'd both signed, and she'd given me a receipt for the $500.00 retainer she'd decided on. There'd been no reaction on her part when I'd pulled a wad of cash out of my pocket and peeled off ten fifty-dollar bills.

"I should probably get a burner phone, huh?" I asked knowingly as she wrote my receipt.

Ms. Abboud looked startled. And possibly amused, although she did her best to hide it.

"Uh, I don't think that will be necessary," she said. "But I'll get you to put my work cell number into your contacts. With a fictitious name, of course."

"What name should I put then?" I asked.

"How about this?" she suggested. She jotted Pipi on a Post-it note and slid it across the desk.

"P. I. P. I," I said as I entered it. "Ah! For private eye!"

"You got it," she said. (I think that might have redeemed me from the question about a burner phone.) "Now, as soon as you can, text me a few good, clear pictures of your dad. And always be sure to delete messages to me as soon as you've sent them."

We worked out the details of how I'd let her know when my dad was supposedly going out of town again. Then I thanked her and left.

It felt strange, walking out of there. Surreal even. I'd just hired a private investigator. To spy on my father.

My *father.*

Suddenly, I couldn't remember why it had seemed so important to find out what he was hiding, or why. I almost went back. Almost told Ms. Abboud to forget the whole thing.

I stood on the sidewalk outside the place for a good ten minutes, torn between going forward or stopping it all right then and there.

In the end, I knew it wasn't going to be possible for me to drop it, to go along as if everything was normal. As I'd told Ms. Abboud — I needed to know the truth.

It's probably not even that bad, I told myself. *And until I have the facts, it's going to creep around in my brain like some dark, lurking monster.*

Her caution echoed in my head all the way home. Whatever I found out was something I would have to carry for the rest of my life.

CHAPTER SEVEN

Twenty minutes and one bus ride later I was back in my neighborhood but not ready to go home. My plan was to grab my bike and get rid of some nervous energy, but before I'd quite reached the house a car stopped at the bottom of my driveway and Owen emerged. His stepmom was at the wheel, and she gave me a quick wave before pulling away.

Owen was just finishing a granola bar and, judging by the way he scowled at the empty wrapper, it hadn't quite done the job.

"This is Dee-Ann's idea of a snack," he said, waving the empty foil pouch. Owen doesn't waste his time on small talk.

"I think we can find you something else," I told him. "Can't have you passing out in our driveway."

"It could happen," he said.

He beat me to the back door, hurried into the kitchen, and started scavenging like a feral cat.

"Is your mom cooking today?" he asked from the inside of the fridge where he'd shoved almost his whole upper body.

"Doesn't look like it," I said. "But stay anyway. She's probably ordering in."

"I'll check to see what's going on at home," he said.

Translation: he was going to find out if his mom's partner, Phil, was going to be home in time for dinner. That probably gives you the impression there are problems at Owen's house. There are, but Phil isn't one of them. Phil is the one who often keeps things from getting too far out of hand.

Owen's mom, who's a genuinely nice person, is also an alcoholic. It's not unusual for her to be a bit blurred by dinnertime, in which case there's no telling what version of her you're going to get. There could be hugs and hilarity, but just as often it'll be hassles and hostility. Sometimes it's a combination — you never know what you're walking into there. I've seen it plenty of times and believe me, it doesn't make mealtime exactly relaxing. Owen avoids eating with her when Phil isn't home.

"Hey, guess what? I was thinking about going back to the gym," Owen told me, emerging from the fridge with a tub of cream cheese dip. "You guys have any chips?"

For the record, Owen has been to the gym exactly twice in the three years I've known him, so he wasn't talking about resuming an inspiring fitness routine. While asking for chips.

I checked the snack cupboard.

"No chips," I said, passing him a box of some kind of snack cracker. "These should work though. So, what made you decide to start hitting the gym again?"

He shrugged. Just as well since he'd already swiped a couple of crackers through the dip and crammed them into his mouth.

I didn't press him, and in any case, it wasn't hard to guess what the answer might be. Most likely, he was interested in someone. About time too. He'd been a mess when his girlfriend of a couple of years moved out west last November. Their plan to stay together long distance hadn't lasted much more than a couple of months and I'd witnessed the misery of him trying to hold onto her while she slowly but surely pulled away. I hoped he was finally ready to put that behind him.

As he munched away on his crackers and dip, my thoughts shifted back to the situation with my dad. I knew I could trust Owen, but just as I was about to fill him in on the strange happenings of the past couple of days, I heard the garage door open.

Dad was home.

I tried to remember if he'd told me how long he'd be "out of town" this time. Sometimes he does but just as often he says it will depend on how long it takes to wrap things up. Whatever that means. More vague and indecipherable talk to go along with the explanations of what it is he actually does.

I've felt a little dim on occasion, when I couldn't follow what he was talking about. Now I suspected that was deliberate. Which made me wonder how much, if *any*, of the stuff he's told me over the years is even true. Heck, maybe it sounded hard to understand because none of it made sense.

Maybe my father was having a secret laugh at me, like he does when he tells clients how he built his business with nothing but hard work and ingenuity and forgets to mention my mother's inheritance.

And then there he was, sauntering into the kitchen, back from his last fictitious business trip.

I watched him as he crossed the room. There was nothing about him, not in his face or movements or the casual way he greeted me and Owen, that seemed off. And yet I knew he'd been lying about where he'd been the past few days, and who knows how many other times. For all I knew, he'd never made a single one of those trips.

It was a strange feeling, looking at my father and knowing he was living some kind of lie. A lie that had infiltrated his own home and family. That thought made me realize something important. I needed to be every bit as smooth as he was. If he thought I suspected anything, it was a sure bet he'd step up whatever precautions he was taking to keep from being found out.

I'd need to be as good at deception as he was. Which was a pretty tall order.

"Sorry I didn't get back to you the other day, Ethan," he said, popping a pod into the coffee maker. "We went straight into meetings, and then it slipped my mind."

"No problem," I said. "I barely remember what I was texting you about."

I almost laughed and added that it couldn't have been too important. But I stopped myself in time because I realized it would sound forced.

It was a weird feeling, as if I was an actor in a play but no one had given me a script.

"Any idea where your mom is?" he asked.

"Not really. She might have mentioned her plans but if she did, I don't remember."

He chuckled at that. Little did he know the reason I'd been so preoccupied all day.

"I'll send her a text," Dad said. "See if she wants me to make reservations for dinner." Then he added, without looking up, "You'll join us, won't you, Owen?"

"I'm not sure — my mom might have cooked," Owen said.

Owen has had plenty of meals at our house, but he doesn't like eating out if it involves any kind of formal dining. I thought I'd better bail him out before anything else was said.

"We'll take a walk to Owen's place and see what's up," I said. "If his mom made dinner I might eat there. Otherwise, maybe we'll just order a pizza or something."

"Whatever you like," Dad said. His voice was casual, but he glanced at me and there was something about his eyes, something *penetrating*, that sent a weird feeling crawling up my neck.

More paranoia? Probably.

All I knew was that I suddenly wanted to be anywhere other than in a room with my father. I grabbed my phone, made sure there was no mess in the kitchen from our snack, and followed Owen out the door.

"Thanks, man," he said.

"Actually, I didn't want to go either," I said.

Owen gave me a curious look. He knows I like eating out, trying new things.

We sure wouldn't be trying anything new at his place, but it was nice to find his mom sober and in the kitchen cooking. Spaghetti sauce, which she makes a lot. It's really good too.

"Hey guys, are ya hungry?"

"Starving," Owen said. The same Owen who'd just eaten half a box of snack crackers and a whole container of dip.

"Honestly. I don't know what that woman has against feeding you properly," she said. "Every time you go to your dad's you come home half malnourished."

"Is Phil here?" Owen asked. He's pretty good at sidestepping criticisms of "that woman," who, of course, is his stepmom, Dee-Ann.

"He's on his way. Have something light if you want — we'll be eating in an hour or so."

"I guess I can wait," Owen said. "We'll be out back."

That sounds like we were heading outside. We weren't. The Cass house has a big sunroom on that end, and it's Owen's favorite place in the house. Over the last couple of years, with his mom's drinking getting worse, it's become a sort of haven to him. He even got interested in the plants out there and spends time fussing over them.

I'm neither here nor there about plants, but I've noticed there's something about that room that makes it a great place for talking. Owen will be going around checking soil and pinching off dead leaves and doing a dozen other plant-tending things, but somehow, he's more able to focus on a conversation there than anywhere else.

So, while he went around doing his thing, I sat in one of the hammock chairs and got started.

"You noticed my dad was just on a business trip, right?"

"Yeah."

"Well, actually, he wasn't. He was right here the whole time."

"What do you mean?" Owen looked puzzled. "He just got home when we were at your place a few minutes ago."

"That's what we're supposed to think. He hasn't been at home — but he wasn't out of town on business either. It was a lie."

"But then, where was he?"

"That's the thing. I have no idea."

The plants were left to fend for themselves as I filled him in on the rest of the details. He interrupted with questions quite a few times — who could blame him, hearing such a bizarre story?

"And you actually hired a spy!" Owen said when I'd finished.

"She's a private investigator," I corrected.

"This is like something in a movie!"

"It kind of is. Doesn't feel real just yet — which is why I'd like to avoid Dad as much as I can for a few days. I'm worried I'll slip up and give something away."

"Right," Owen said. "I'll have to be careful too."

"You'll be fine," I said. More accurately, Dad always finds Owen a little quirky, so not much he did was likely to get Dad's attention.

Owen isn't quirky, by the way. Maybe a bit socially awkward sometimes but that's true of lots of people.

And as for me, I figured I could carry it off. All I had to do was be careful not to do anything to raise his suspicions.

Little did I know I already had.

CHAPTER EIGHT

Breakfast the next morning was absolutely normal. Not a hint, not a sign, not a single reason to worry.

It was afterward, when I was about to get ready to meet up with Nora, that Dad mentioned it was pickup day.

"I have a few things to go in the recycling bin if you wouldn't mind taking them out for me, Ethan."

"Sure."

"They're in my storage office," he said, pushing back from the table. For a minute he stood there, finishing his coffee. Then he told Mom he'd be working at home today and maybe they could tackle something on her never-ending home project list if he found some free time.

"I'd love to get that new squirrel-proof bird feeder up," Mom said.

It's cute how excited she gets when they're going to do something like that together. You'd think it was some kind of married couple date.

Dad leaned down, smiling, and kissed her nose as he passed by her place at the table.

"Poor squirrels," he said. He winked at me.

The stomach lurch I'd felt at the mention of the "storage office" began to calm. As I followed him down the stairs and along the hall leading to it, I reminded myself that none of this was cause for alarm. He worked at home on a regular basis. And "bin management," as Dad put it, was my job.

"Forgot to ask you," he said as he punched in the door codes, "how'd you like the new bike?"

"It's great," I said. "Thanks."

"Good, good." He stepped into the room. "Just grab those boxes over there."

On the right there was a small stack of broken-down boxes, tied with a piece of twine. I didn't remember seeing it when I'd been in there the other day, but then I'd had other things on my mind.

"Probably a while since you were in this dusty place," Dad said.

And then I knew that *he* knew.

It was a test of nerves I wasn't ready for. Except, I had no choice.

"Actually," I said, picking up the boxes, keeping my voice steady, "I was in here the other day."

"Oh, yeah?" He barely sounded interested. "Looking for something?"

"Not really. I just wanted the key for your office."

"My office? What for?" His voice and his expression offered nothing but a hint of curiosity. No alarm. No suspicion.

It was chilling. I knew he must have seen the charge for the Uber drive and realized I'd been to his office. This whole conversation was a charade, to see if I had something to hide.

I had to persuade him it was innocent.

"It was kind of dumb," I said. "When I texted you — there'd been a fight with Nora and me, I dunno, just wanted to talk for a minute."

"Bad timing," he said. "I'm sorry about that."

"No, it's okay." I tried to look sheepish, which wasn't all that hard because lying that way made me feel like an idiot. "Anyway, I got this crazy idea to go to your office, like it might calm me. As if there'd be a sense of your presence or something."

He smiled. "And was there?"

"Not really. But I think it helped, the empty space and quiet."

"And how are things with Nora now?"

"We're okay. It was one of those things that gets blown out of proportion."

That he'd have no trouble believing. And I was ninety percent certain he'd bought the whole thing.

Or — was it possible my suspicions were completely unfounded? Could I have imagined there was anything more to any of this than a normal father-son exchange? How could I be sure, either way?

The truth was, I *couldn't*. Which meant I had to stay vigilant until I had proof one way or the other. And act totally natural at the same time.

I nodded at the boxes I was holding. "Is this it?" I asked.

"That's it, for now," he said.

"K," I said. "Well, I'm meeting Nora, so —"

He gave me a one-swipe wave and I left.

As I tucked the boxes in among all the other stuff in the bin a moment later, I mentally congratulated myself. Which felt strange. "Good job, Ethan. You're turning out to be quite the accomplished liar."

Not the kind of praise I ever expected to be giving myself, even if it *was* something I'd been forced into doing. And some of it had been the result of my dad's own words.

"Never oversell, Ethan," he'd told me on more than one occasion. "The biggest mistake people make when they're trying to hustle someone is talking too much. Let them draw information out of you. Otherwise, you seem too eager, and eager looks guilty, or desperate."

I wondered how he'd like it, knowing I'd taken his advice and used it against him. The urge to make my story more believable by adding extra details had been strong, but I'd fought it. Successfully, it seemed.

I heard a thump against the garage door as I was wheeling my bike — the new Trek, so Dad wouldn't wonder why I'd use the old one instead — toward the side entrance. As I rounded the corner at the front I found Owen, shooting hoops.

"Hey," I said. "I'm meeting Nora, but I'll walk the bike as far as your place if you want."

He tossed the ball back into the deck box and fell in beside me. "How's everything going?"

"Good. I think I did okay covering up why I went to his office. So, as long as I don't make any more dumb mistakes like I did taking Ubers, I should be in the clear."

"Just don't tell Nora about any of this," Owen cautioned.

I said nothing. Looked straight ahead and kept walking.

"Oh, man. It's too late, isn't it?" he said.

"She won't say anything," I said. I was glad we'd almost reached his house.

"She won't say anything," he repeated. There was no doubting his tone. "You have got to be kidding. The second she gets mad at you, she's unpredictable. How do you not know that yet?"

"She wouldn't mess me up over something big like this," I said.

Owen threw his hands up. "I hope you're right," he said. And then he let it go.

That's the way he is. He'll tell you what he thinks but he won't go on and on the way some people do. We disagree on a regular basis, but it never turns into anything you'd call an actual fight.

He tapped me on the shoulder and said he'd see me later, but he didn't move, which made me think he wasn't going back into his house. I wondered if it was a bad morning. That's not unusual, and although his mom had been sober at suppertime yesterday, that didn't mean she'd stayed that way. I've been around in the mornings for some pretty tense scenes, especially if she wakes up hungover and Phil is in a foul mood over whatever went on the night before.

Knowing that made me feel a little guilty as I stood on the pedals and started toward Nora's. Owen doesn't have a long list of friends and I know I'm the only one he's close enough with to talk to about certain things.

Nora was waiting, all smiles and joy.

"Notice anything different?" she asked, twirling around, arms lifted.

"Did you get your hair cut?"

"No!" She giggled.

"Is it something you're wearing? Because you know I don't notice much about clothes."

"It's not clothes, silly. I know you're hopeless in that department."

She'd stopped twirling and stepped closer. I stopped trying to figure out what I'd missed when she snaked her arms around my neck and lifted her face to look me in the eyes.

"Do you want me to keep making hopeless guesses, or kiss you?" I asked.

She opted for the kiss. Then she told me what I hadn't noticed.

"I'm all tanned!"

She tugged free and did another twirl.

"Looks great," I said. "But you always look great. Except that time you drank all your dad's beer and I had to hold your hair out of the way while you were heaving behind the shed."

She laughed and gave me a playful swat.

"We need to make plans," she said. "How about a swim?"

"Sure. I'll have to grab a pair of trunks first. Beach or pool?"

"Crestview," she said, which surprised me. The Crestview pool is closer, but she loves the beach at Mooney's Bay.

When we pulled our bikes up to my place Nora decided she'd wait outside to avoid getting trapped in a conversation with one of my parents. I admit I was relieved. Even before Owen's warning earlier I'd been regretting telling her about my father. She wouldn't give anything away on purpose, but I could picture her asking Dad some "innocent" question about his weekend, which he'd see through in a heartbeat.

"Back in a sec," I told her, before she could change her mind.

"Grab an extra towel too," she said. "I forgot mine."

As we pedaled toward Crestview, I made a comment about my mom, and how busy she is all the time, even though she doesn't have a job.

"Must be hard for your mom to keep up with things sometimes," I said, hoping it didn't seem like a weird thing to bring up.

If it was, Nora missed it. She did what I was hoping she'd do, which was get talking about her mother. A lot of it was the usual grievances. Her mom never has time to do things with her. Her mom is in a bad mood a lot. That kind of thing.

But she also talked about her mom's job, which was why I'd brought the subject up.

"She's always complaining about how she's not paid enough, and people don't appreciate her. On and on. I told her if she hates it that much she should quit, but that just made her mad."

"She's a nurse, right?" I asked.

"No, she does something in administration," she said. "Good thing too. Imagine being sick and having my mom take care of you."

I filed that bit of information away just as we arrived at the pool.

It was a great day. The weather was perfect but even so the pool wasn't crowded. The sun on the water created a mosaic that sparkled and shifted, and Nora moved through it like a sea nymph. Her eyes were bright and every time they met mine the smile that followed made my chest ache.

I even managed to overcome the pulse of fear that almost always haunts happy moments with Nora. Maybe that was because there was a different threat hovering, although I didn't know if it had anywhere near as much power to hurt.

CHAPTER NINE

By midweek I was pretty well smoothed out. I'd adjusted to the shock of my dad's deception, and the inner tension when I was around him had settled. Most importantly, I felt confident I was acting natural. There were no signs he suspected I knew a thing.

My ability to carry it off was made easier by the fact that whenever we happened to be in the same room together, everything genuinely felt normal. Sometimes I almost wondered if I'd dreamt the whole thing.

While I wanted (needed) to know what was going on, part of me hoped it would be weeks before the next so-called business trip. That wasn't a realistic wish though. When Dad had first started having meetings "out-of-town" it had been once, maybe twice a month. Now it wasn't unusual for him to be away for a few days three or even four times a month. So, I knew there was a good chance the next trip would be soon, and I wasn't wrong.

It was on Sunday, at the dinner table, that Dad mentioned he'd be leaving for "business meetings" the next morning and probably wouldn't be back until the following Monday at the earliest.

I wanted to know what time his pretend flight was so I could alert Ms. Abboud, but I'd never asked anything like that before and was afraid to risk it. Luckily, Mom spoke up.

"What time do you leave for the airport?"

"Nine-thirty or so," he said.

I picked up the dinner plates and cutlery and took them to the kitchen — to demonstrate my lack of interest while I listened carefully to every word.

"That's okay then. I think I'm blocking your car, but I'll be heading out a good hour before that."

I finished clearing the table, loaded the dishwasher, and looked around to see if there were any stray cups I'd missed before tossing in a soap pod and hitting the start button. By then, Dad had disappeared down into his "storage office" and Mom was scrolling through one of the streaming programs she subscribes to.

"You in the mood to watch something?" she asked. A courtesy, not an indication that she wanted company — our combined TV viewing, when it happens, is always a compromise for one of us. Not exactly enjoyable. I passed.

I wished Nora was free, but she'd picked up a couple of extra shifts this week after one of her co-workers called in sick. And Owen has a regular Sunday thing with an online gaming group — something he's tried unsuccessfully to persuade me to join at least a dozen times. I'm a decent enough player, but I've never been keen on the idea of locking myself in on a regular schedule, especially with people I don't know.

Anyway, before I made any plans, I needed to let "Pipi" know about my dad's plans for the morning. Her answer to my text was back quickly and it was good news. Her Monday morning was flexible, so she'd be ready to follow him when he left the house.

It felt strange, like a surge of power and fear running through me at the same time. I might be on the verge of solving the mystery of my father's secret life.

Just what I was going to do with that information, I had no idea. I'd been so fixated on wondering what he was up to, that I hadn't given any serious thought to how I'd handle it if I found out he was involved in something sleazy.

I shook off that thought and headed out on my bike looking for something to do. It only took a few minutes. There was a cluster of kids I knew from school messing around with a soccer ball in a sports field not far from my place. I joined in for a while, but my performance was lousy. Too much on my mind. No one on the impromptu team I'd been part of protested when I decided to leave.

The next morning brought a sense of dread. And guilt, when Dad slipped me three twenties and a fifty, "in case I needed anything." I told him thanks even as I was thinking, *Yeah, I might need a cab or two, or something else to keep you from tracking my movements.*

That last part echoed in my head after he'd left. *Tracking my movements.*

It's an interesting thing, suspicion. As soon as the thought came to me that my father could be keeping tabs on me, flashbacks started popping up in my brain. Casual questions he'd asked that put me in the position of telling him things I might have preferred not to. I'd usually told the truth, or some version of it, but there had been times I'd decided to make something up instead. Not even because I had anything significant to hide, but there were certain things I figured were my business. A person can have perfectly innocent reasons for keeping something private.

But now I see it's a possibility — a probability even, that he knew when I was lying. That he already knew where I'd been every time he'd asked me. It gave me the creeps.

I waited, on edge, all day, avoiding everyone. It wasn't until midafternoon that I heard from Ms. Abboud. She texted to say she could see me at four o'clock if I was able to come in.

When I got there, she was standing in the doorway of her personal office, talking to a man I assumed was the "Rayne" part of Abboud and Rayne. When she saw me, she signaled me inside right away. Her face told me nothing, which I suppose is a good trait in a private investigator.

Once we were both seated, she asked me how I was. A standard courtesy, but I was in no mood for small talk.

"Good. Fine," I said. And because I didn't want to look rude, I made myself ask the same of her.

"I'm well, thank you," she said. Without wasting any more time, she pushed a file across the table to me, nodding for me to have a look.

The first item I saw when I flipped the folder jacket open was a photo of three men. One was my father.

As I studied the picture, Ms. Abboud began to speak.

"I followed your father from your home to a second location marked as number one on the attached map — it's the last page in the file you have."

I slid the map out and quickly found the number one.

"That's where I saw him last week," I said.

She nodded to acknowledge she'd heard me before continuing.

"Your dad parked his car in a lot behind the building there, which left it quite hidden from the street. He joined two other gentlemen at that time, as you see in Exhibit A."

There was nothing written on the photo of the three men but when I flipped it over and checked the back, I saw it had been stamped with the word *Exhibit* and an *A* was written in by hand.

"A dark, chauffeur-driven sedan was waiting in front of the strip mall, and the three men got in. During my observations, there didn't appear to be any conversation between the passengers and the driver. You can see the driver in the next photo, which is Exhibit B."

She paused while I looked that picture over.

"Do you recognize any of these men as the ones you saw your father with at this location previously? Or the gentleman you observed in the lobby of your father's office building the following day?"

"They could be the same guys from the parking lot; I'm not sure. I didn't really pay much attention to them." I looked closer and pointed to the tallest man. "This *might* be the guy from the lobby, but I only looked at him for a second or two."

"Understandable," Ms. Abboud said. "Anyway, I was able to follow the sedan undetected — there was no indication from the driver that he was watching for a tail. The car left the city, going west on 31, exiting on Davidson, and taking various rural roads as indicated on the map."

Ms. Abboud had marked it clearly with a pink highlighter. Finding my way there wouldn't be a problem. Transportation would. I pulled my attention back to what she was saying.

"They stopped at location number two, here." She leaned forward and tapped the spot on the map. "It's marked by a small painted sign that just says Welcome, so nothing helpful there."

I nodded to let Ms. Abboud know I was following, and she continued.

"There's a residence there, set back off the road, with a privacy hedge in front. I didn't see anyone getting out of the car because they parked in the attached garage.

"However, I turned back a bit farther along, and was able to get a look at the place by pulling off the road and making my way close to it under cover of a patch of trees on the north side of the building. It appears to be a single-family home. Nice, but not overly conspicuous. There's a photo. Exhibit C."

She passed me a picture of the place. Just a regular house, like she'd described.

"From that vantage point, I discovered that the hedge along the front hides a small parking area directly in front of the house. Room enough for two or three cars. In fact, while I was there, a woman in a small white car drove in, parked, and went inside. She was only there for a few moments before she re-emerged and left. I got a picture but it's unclear because a light mist had started to fall. Exhibits D and E."

I lifted the photo from the folder. It was true, the details of that photo were blurred.

"About fifteen minutes later, two other vehicles pulled in," Ms. Abboud said. "An elderly couple, and a man with a child. Photos were impossible by then, and anyway it was time for me to go. I didn't mind the rain, but one has to be careful in a rural setting. I needed to move along before my car drew unwelcome attention."

It seemed her report was finished. I shuffled through the photos and map again and saw that there was also an envelope in there containing a printout of the report she'd just given verbally.

"So, what do you think is going on?" I asked.

"At this point, I could only guess, and that's something I generally avoid."

"But you have an idea, don't you?"

"Even if I do, an idea is just an idea. I like to deal in facts and reasonable certainty."

"So then, is there any way you can find out? For sure?"

"Not without getting inside that house. Even attempting such a thing, say by pretending to be lost or whatever, would be risky. Anything that made them suspicious could prompt them to shut down the operation or find a new location. It's not worth taking a chance of that happening."

I knew I couldn't suggest anything illegal, like trying to get inside when there was no one there, but another thought occurred to me.

"Can't you spy, like with a telescope or something?" I asked.

Ms. Abboud smiled. "It's not quite as simple as that. Without sound, you could run that kind of surveillance for days and find out nothing. And there's the problem of having to leave a vehicle somewhere along the road. You might as well drop a note in their mailbox telling them someone is nearby with eyes on them."

I realized then that a person with Ms. Abboud's experience would already have considered every possibility, which left me feeling kind of deflated.

"So, I won't be able to find out what's going on in there?"

"I'm not saying there's nothing else I could try, but the risk of raising their suspicions is much stronger than the likelihood of learning anything through a cold walk in. I just can't recommend it."

"I understand," I said, but I know she could see the disappointment on my face.

"Look, Ethan," she said, "it's probable — but not certain — that there's an illegal operation of some sort taking place. And that could make any further digging dangerous. I know this isn't what you want to hear, but I believe it's best you leave it at that, at least for now. Wait for other opportunities to present themselves."

I took that in. I knew she was giving me good, solid advice.

And I knew I wasn't going to take it.

If she couldn't go any further looking into what my father was up to, I was going to find a way to do it on my own.

CHAPTER TEN

Judging by everything Ms. Abboud had done, and the time it had taken her, I'd expected a pretty hefty final bill. It was a surprise then when she told me we were all square.

"But —" I shuffled the papers she'd given me, looking back and forth at them and her. "You spent a lot of time on this."

"I applied the student discount," she said, managing not to smile. It wasn't hard to guess I was the only student who'd ever hired her.

"Well, thanks a lot," I said. "I really appreciate everything you did."

"That's what I'm here for," she said lightly. She reached a hand forward then and shook mine.

"Good luck, Ethan. I hope this all works out okay."

I thanked her again, took the folder of evidence she'd given me, and was soon on my bike, heading toward home. I was almost there when I remembered I was supposed to meet Nora at her house when she'd finished her shift. I was going to be late anyway, so I decided to stop by my place to put the folder somewhere safe. The saddlebags on my bike aren't exactly secure. Maybe if I didn't keep losing the locks …

Plus, I was hungry. I slapped together a sandwich and ate it in my room while I considered the best hiding spot for my *evidence.* I knew I'd want to look some of it over again, so I eliminated ideas like taping it to the underside of a drawer. After a bit of thought I decided to hide it in plain sight, so to speak. I had an old boot box in my closet where I kept achievement certificates and a couple of third place trophies from track and field. They'd been sitting up there on the back corner of the shelf, pretty much undisturbed for a few years. I pulled it down, lifted out the trophies, slid the file folder underneath the papers, and stuck it all back in place. I could access it anytime and knew the chance anyone would ever go looking through it was basically nil.

It was almost an hour later when I finally connected with Nora. She'd eaten with her mom and sister and was waiting for me at her place. Waiting *impatiently*, according to her text message, which she backed up with five exclamation marks. I shot back a quick note that I was on my way. Luckily, it's only a few minutes' bike ride from here to there.

Nora was at the kitchen table when I got there. Her back was to me, so I tapped on the door, said, "Hey," and stepped inside. A small machine sat on the table in front of her. I'd seen it one other time, so I knew it had something to do with nail polish. I should have known what it did since she'd given me a long and detailed explanation, but I couldn't remember a single thing about it.

As I took the chair closest to her, she finished applying polish to her left thumbnail and stuck her thumb into the nail machine. She pressed a button, and a light came on.

"You took forever getting here so I thought I might as well do my nails," she said.

"Yeah, sure. Sorry I was late." I leaned in. "I had to go meet with the private investigator."

That got her interest.

"Really? So, what did you find out?" The machine clicked off and she pulled out her thumb, put in a couple of fingers and pressed the button again.

"Turns out it was nothing. Some schedule mix-up and a later flight. No big mystery at all."

"You're so paranoid," she said with a laugh. "And here you thought he was hiding some deep, dark secret."

"I felt like some kind of a crackpot when she told me."

Nora was focused on her nails again, which was a good thing for me. I feel really guilty lying to her, and that makes me terrible at it. It's like I have an inbuilt auto-response waiting to send her signals. And sure enough, heat began crawling up my neck and across my face. I knew I was getting red, something Nora would have spotted if she hadn't been so engrossed in her nails.

"Well, it's good everything was okay after all," she said, tapping impatiently on the table with her free hand.

The machine beeped and she pulled out the final two fingers and held her hand up for inspection.

"That's it for the undercoating," she said.

I didn't know what that meant but it definitely didn't sound like she was finished. That gave me a chance to escape for a few minutes.

"I'm just gonna use the bathroom," I said, and got out of there before she happened to register the guilt on my face and neck.

It was worse than I'd expected. The face in the mirror over the sink was nothing short of a confession. Red blotches that made me look as if I'd been attacked by a mini paintball gun — they might as well have spelled out LIAR. I shuddered to think of what the rest of the night would have been like if Nora had noticed.

Turning on the cold water, I wet my hands and patted my face and neck over and over. At the same time, I took slow, deep breaths to help settle the thumping in my chest. I didn't return to the kitchen until my color was back to normal.

However long that had taken, it hadn't been enough time for Nora to finish with her nails. I hid my impatience for the next twenty minutes while she did a bunch of mysterious things, many of which involved further use of the machine.

"Aren't they gorgeous?" she asked when she was finally finished. She waved her fingertips in the air in front of my face.

"Really nice," I said. "You ready to head out now?"

"Why? Are you in a hurry all of a sudden, after getting here late?"

"No hurry," I said.

"I still have to get changed," she said pointedly.

I knew she was taking her time because I'd made her wait, but the guilt for lying was lingering, so I let it go. Still, it annoyed me. It's not like I'd been late on purpose, and she was making it pretty clear that she was dragging her feet deliberately.

I don't know if it was that or what, but I had a lousy time at the pool party. If you could call it a party.

It's hard to figure out what makes some parties so fun and others so lame. You can have the same basic group of people, music, munchies, and everything else, and yet one night it will be a blast and another night it feels dull and almost depressing.

I know I talked to people. But in a strange way it was as if I was watching a cast of strangers on a screen.

Maybe that was the whole problem. It wasn't my mood, or Nora, or my dad at all. Maybe it was just one of those nights when nothing sparks to life. It was as if we were trying, like it was a rehearsal for a play nobody cared about, but we kept saying our lines and going through the motions.

Nora commented on it when we were walking to her place afterward.

"I don't know why, but that wasn't even fun."

I gave her hand a squeeze.

"Just one of those things, I guess," I said.

She turned then, kind of jerking my arm with the sudden movement. Facing me she stepped closer. She put her hands on either side of my face and tugged my mouth toward hers.

No argument from me. I drew her close and as we kissed everything bad disappeared. She made those "Mmm" sounds and I wished we were somewhere private.

"I'm sorry I was a jerk about waiting for you," she said when we resumed walking.

"A jerk — how?" I said. I knew, of course, but why risk spoiling the moment? I've seen that happen before. If I seemed to agree she'd been out of line earlier, there would likely be an argument.

One time an apology actually turned into a breakup. No joke. When we finally made up, she explained to me that it only happened because she's more sensitive than most people. (I told that to Owen and he snorted apple juice out his nose.)

"I guess you didn't catch it," Nora said. "But I did my nails because you made me wait. Like a revenge thing. Sorry."

"Well, your nails look great," I said, staying neutral. "Hey, are you guys still having company tomorrow?"

"Yes, my uncle and cousins," she said. "It's Uncle Teddy's birthday. The first one since his wife died. So, we want to make it really special."

"Makes sense," I said, though I wasn't sure about that. It probably depended on what their idea of "making it really special" was.

"We might be able to hang out tomorrow night if he doesn't stay too late," Nora said. "I mean, I don't want to ruin your weekend."

"Don't worry about that," I said. "I'll find something else to do."

"With Owen, I suppose," she said. Owen isn't her favorite person. No doubt she's picked up on his opinion of her, though he does his best to be nice whenever we're all together.

I didn't say anything about that but my plans for Saturday weren't about Owen. Dad had said he'd be "gone" until Monday at least, so that gave me the whole weekend to do ... exactly what, I wasn't sure, but I planned to figure it out.

We'd reached Nora's place by then. We sat out on the back deck for a while, although I never like that much. Nora's folks peek out the windows at us whenever we're there, which I find creepy. She and I will be talking and all of a sudden, we'll become aware of the curtain moving slowly away from the side of a window. And then an eyeball will appear in the crack.

If one of us looks over, the curtain will shut in a flash. Otherwise, in a couple of minutes it will creep closed just as slowly as it opened. Once they're satisfied we're not doing whatever it is they think they might catch us doing with their super shifty surveillance.

My parents would never, in a million years, pull a stunt like that. On the other hand, every time — and I mean *every* time —

Nora is over and we go to hang out in my room, Mom makes a point of telling me to keep the door open.

You've got to wonder what any of that is supposed to accomplish.

CHAPTER ELEVEN

It was drizzling on Friday morning. A good chance to strategize, I decided, as if I hadn't lain awake half the night trying to think of how to overcome the obstacles Ms. Abboud had described to me yesterday. If they were problems for someone with her experience, not to mention a car, it looked pretty hopeless for me.

While I waited for a brilliant idea to strike, a text popped up from Owen saying he was heading for the gym. Lishan's Athletics. Did I want to go?

I wasn't in the mood, so I answered that I'd go another time. But a while later I got feeling guilty and decided to meet him there.

Lishan's Athletics isn't the closest fitness place to us, but it's got some cool stuff you don't find at traditional clubs.

Owen was already there when I arrived. He was talking to one of the staff members, a girl named Kylie who seemed to possess an endless supply of enthusiasm. She was speaking as I got close enough to hear.

"So, it doesn't *matter* if you haven't been working out regularly — it's *never* too late to start. We can set up a routine for you to follow on your own, or you can work with one of our personal trainers."

"I don't know about a personal trainer," Owen said.

"It's a great way to keep yourself motivated, especially when you're getting started," Kylie said.

"I guess I could try it," Owen said.

"Sounds *great*! Now, let me see who's available today."

"Ethan!" Owen blurted, spying me.

Kylie blinked hard a couple of times.

"Uh, we don't have a trainer named Ethan," she said.

"No, that's Ethan," Owen said. He pointed at me with a grin.

"I don't believe we allow people to bring in their own trainers," Kylie said. She gave me a quick, rueful smile, which I noticed was coupled with a decidedly skeptical scan of my physique.

"No, no. Ethan's just a friend," Owen said. He could have quit there but nope. He laughed and added, "I mean, he's obviously not a trainer."

I managed what I hoped was a good-natured smile.

Kylie didn't manage to hide her relief, but she moved on quickly, looking around and signaling a guy who'd been tossing a tire end over end like it was made of Styrofoam.

He sauntered over, introduced himself as Rohan, shook Owen's hand, and glanced at me.

"Were you looking for a trainer too?"

"No, I'm good," I said, which might have been a poor choice of words considering the way his eyebrows lifted.

"Sure, yeah, well, anytime you change your mind —"

He left that hanging and turned his attention back to Owen. I did a low-key workout while Rohan got Owen set up with a training schedule. It looked like things were going well any time I glanced their way.

More than an hour later, we stepped back outside. The shower had stopped, and the sun was blasting down ferocious waves of heat, turning the fallen rain to steam. It was difficult to breathe, and my back and forehead were instantly slick with sweat.

Owen was trying to be subtle about checking his biceps when a car pulled up and three guys got out. They were on their way to the gym door when the one who'd been driving stopped and looked at me.

"Hey," he said. "You're Ethan, right?"

"Right," I said. "Uh, sorry — do I know you?"

"We were in the same class in grade seven," he said. "Aki Hirano."

"Aki!" I said. "I didn't recognize you, sorry."

"No one does," he said, grinning. "I've changed a bit."

A bit was an understatement. The Aki I'd known back then barely resembled the guy standing outside the gym. The new version was taller, filled out, and had lost all of the awkwardness of a middle grader.

We hadn't been friends back then, not in the real sense of the word. On friendly terms, sure, but aside from group things we'd never actually hung out. So, our conversation outside the gym was just one of those polite things. Except, it didn't end there.

It turned out Aki was the cousin of a girl named Kasumi from our neighborhood — one who'd been involved in a tragic event a year ago. It was Owen who mentioned the last name connection and the next thing I knew we were in the middle of this heavy talk about that terrible day.

I was never much into the drug scene. Sure, I'd shared a joint now and then, but it wasn't really my thing. Then, last summer, seven kids from school had a small backyard gathering a couple of streets over. Firepit, music, a hang-out kind of thing. One of the girls had brought along what the papers reported she'd described as "killer weed."

That particular quote was told to a journalist by the lone survivor. The other six kids didn't make it. It turned out the weed was heavily laced with fentanyl, something the guy who'd sold it had kept to himself. If he even knew about it, that is. He's waiting to go to trial on six counts of manslaughter and will probably get some serious time, which is still a better fate than the kids who ended up splayed around the firepit, staring sightlessly into the night sky. The fire was still smoldering when the survivor was finally able to move enough to get help.

Six dead kids. Ordinary kids, goofing around one minute; living, breathing, *being*, and then gone in an instant. Their pictures were in all the papers, and it gave me a kind of crawling feeling looking at them. One of the girls had the prettiest eyes you ever saw — they shone with life and laughter. It haunted me for months, the thought of how empty those eyes must have looked at the end. Still and vacant.

The effect on the community was, as you can imagine, paralyzing. For weeks, people moved and spoke and even seemed to breathe in a heavy, subdued way.

It chilled me, knowing if I'd been there, I'd have done exactly what the rest of them had done. The thought jumped into my brain at the oddest times: *That could have been me.* One toke *and that could have been me.*

Unlike Aki, I'd had no real connection to any of the victims, and seeing the sorrow he was carrying was hard. It was clear he'd been close to Kasumi. One of the six victims.

When we'd finished talking, I told him he should drop by sometime. It's the kind of thing you might say to be polite, but I meant it. Even so, it was a surprise when the very next morning he showed up at my door.

"This is a bit awkward," he said before I could speak, "but would you have an iPad I could borrow for this evening?"

It was an odd request, considering. I didn't want to answer it either way without finding out more.

"Come on in," I said, stepping back to let him by and then taking him to the kitchen.

"Want a bottle of juice or pop? Or a coffee maybe?"

Once we were seated, drinks in front of us, Aki explained.

"I do event photography — and I guess I'm okay at it because I get pretty regular work." He took a sip of coffee. "Anyway, I got a last-minute booking for tonight, but my tablet is in for repair. So —"

I didn't make him ask again. And after I'd agreed to lend him my tablet, he told me a bit more about his photography business. He'd built it up quite by accident after a friend's mom saw some of his casual photos. And now he was doing well enough that he'd bought himself a car.

I'd assumed he'd been driving a family car when I'd seen him at the gym, but it was his. Bought with money he made taking photos at events!

I suck at taking pictures. Like, seriously. You could put the world's best camera in my hands and it wouldn't help. So I was curious enough to check my cloud and scroll through the images he took that evening.

They were fantastic. Original and real and intriguing, in shot after shot it was like he'd captured images most of us would miss. I must have spent hours looking at those pictures.

I could hardly wait to talk to him about them when he brought my iPad back the next morning.

CHAPTER TWELVE

It's weird how sometimes you just know you can trust somebody. I got that with Aki right away. First when I was passing over my iPad, and again when he brought it back and we got talking. Even so, I surprised myself when I suddenly asked if I could tell him something private and trust him to keep it to himself.

"Of course," he said.

I liked that. Just, "Of course," like it was the most natural and obvious answer. I'd have been wary if he'd tried to sell me on how trustworthy he was.

The next minute I was telling him the whole story of seeing my father in the city when he was pretending to be away, hiring Ms. Abboud, and everything else.

Again, I liked his reaction. He didn't make a big or little deal of it. He just listened, nodding to let me know he was taking it in. When I'd finished talking, he only had one thing to say.

"Is there anything I can do to help?"

That was more than I'd hoped for. I'd been trying to think of the best way to ask if he'd be willing to get involved. Never crossed my mind he'd just up and offer.

So, I told him what I'd like him to do, making sure it was clear I expected to pay for his time and costs. And I told him if he agreed, I needed to trust him to keep what he was doing one hundred percent confidential. Because a single slip could end up blowing the whole thing.

Aki thrust his hand forward and shook mine, which was a bit odd and formal but also felt like it meant something.

"Count on it," he said. And then, surprising me again, he added, "So, would right now be a good time to start?"

"Seriously?"

"Why not? Honestly, and I don't mean to make light of the situation — I realize this is serious, but it's also something different and interesting to do."

That was true, although it was "something different and interesting" I'd have preferred not to be doing. Even so, I was with him as far as getting started right away and was about to tell him so, when a familiar tap-tap tap-tap at the door jerked me back to reality.

Nora!

In the surprise of Aki turning up, and the distraction of the conversation we'd had, I'd forgotten that Nora's parents were dropping her off at my place after lunch.

A moment later she was standing in the room looking back and forth between me and Aki while I gave a slightly garbled explanation that he was someone from my old neighborhood, and that we'd just reconnected.

"Right, well, nice to meet you, Aki," she said. "And I'm sorry to break up this reunion or whatever, but we have plans this afternoon, right Ethan?"

"We do," I said. "Maybe we can pick this up later, Aki."

He agreed and stood to go but I didn't want him to leave before we got a few things settled.

"Oh, um, before you go, let me, uh, show you that, um, that thing we were talking about — it's in my room," I said. As I spoke, I could feel Nora's eyes boring into me. And who could blame her the way I'd just babbled out a string of words?

Aki followed me upstairs, down the hall and into my bedroom, grinning the entire way.

"What's so funny?" I asked.

"Your girlfriend is going to have a few questions for you when I leave," he said, barely suppressing a laugh.

I managed a weak smile. Then I gave him the location Ms. Abboud had followed my dad and the others to, and we exchanged phone numbers to connect later.

"I'll take a drive out there and have a look around in the meantime," he told me. "And don't worry — I'll stay out of sight."

"Perfect." I pulled the money Dad had given me on Monday out of my pocket. "Here's $110 for gas and toward your time. You can think about what you'll charge per hour, and we'll talk later today."

Aki looked at the money. He hesitated for a couple of seconds before taking it. "Text me when you're free," he said.

He was not wrong about Nora. The door was hardly closed behind him when she started.

"You want to tell me what's going on, Ethan?"

"What? Nothing's 'going on,'" I claimed. "I told you; Aki and I ran into each other at the gym yesterday when I was there with Owen. I think Owen's interested in someone because he's got this sudden urge to work out."

"Don't try to change the subject," she warned. "What was that business about showing this guy something in your room? I mean, it was obviously a lie, but what were you doing up there?"

"I just wanted to tell him something," I said. I felt suddenly tired, like my brain couldn't handle the long interrogation I knew was coming. Nora can be relentless.

"Like what? Is there some big secret you can't share with your own girlfriend, or are you hiding something from me?"

"No big secret," I said. "And if there was one, it wouldn't follow that it had anything to do with you at all."

"So there *is* something!"

"I said there wasn't."

"But you're obviously lying. You've been lying since I walked in the door today. Why do you do that?"

"I don't do that. Can we just drop this whole thing and have a nice afternoon together like we planned?"

"No. I don't think we can. Not if you're going to lie and hide things from me. How am I supposed to enjoy my time with you when you're being such a jerk?"

"Come on, Nora," I said. "Can you please let it go for once?"

"Maybe that's what I should do," she said. She stood, facing me with her eyes blazing and her jaw set in a hard line. "Maybe I should let this whole relationship go."

I was so sick of this kind of argument. Fights over nothing. And I knew what was coming. I'd seen the signs often enough to know what they meant.

Except, this time, I didn't wait for her to say it. From somewhere outside of everything I feel for this girl, I pulled together the strength to speak first.

"Maybe you should," I said.

For a couple of seconds, we stood there, facing each other, frozen. And then her face crumpled, and I wished I could grab those words back and hold her. Except, she was already moving toward the door and before I could say or do a single thing she paused to turn and hiss her favorite phrase in this kind of situation.

"I hate you."

Nice. But weirdly, it didn't feel like a stab in the gut this time. Man, the first time she ever said that I almost couldn't breathe from the way it hit me. Maybe I'd become immune.

The door closed behind her with the expected bang, which would have alerted Mom if she'd been home. I was glad she wasn't. The whole on and off thing with Nora really bothered her. I'd learned to hide it from my parents when it was happening if I could.

It struck me that I no longer knew how many times Nora had broken up with me. It had become her automatic reaction to practically any argument we had, and I realized that was why I was standing there feeling almost indifferent.

It had become so normal, so routine, that I just assumed we'd patch things up whenever it happened.

No wonder Owen made snarky comments. And offered annoying, unsolicited advice. Such as: "She might knock it off if you didn't crawl back to her every time." And: "You seriously need to man up, bro."

Pep talks by Owen.

I realized I was standing there staring at the door, like she might come back and say she hadn't meant it. As if that ever happened.

In any case, it wasn't something I wanted to think about then. And Nora would need cooling off time before I could even try to talk to her. That meant my day was suddenly freed up.

I texted Aki. *Change of plans. Can you come back for me?*

He pulled into the driveway less than ten minutes later, which gave me time to throw some snacks and drinks into a backpack. I was waiting for him at the door because Mom had texted to say she'd be home soon, and I didn't want her to meet Aki. The mistakes I'd made when I'd gone to Dad's office had shown me the importance of being super cautious. For the time being, any contact between Aki and my parents was potentially risky.

I slid into the passenger seat and clicked my belt as he backed onto the street. I was half expecting him to ask about what had happened with Nora and was glad he didn't.

"What do you think," he said. "Should we start by taking a drive by the place?"

"Definitely. We need to do a little recon before we can put a plan together."

"A *little recon*?" he said. His mouth twitched but he didn't smile.

I laughed at my attempt to sound smooth, and Aki quickly joined me.

It was a badly needed release of tension, for me anyway.

The drive to the address Ms. Abboud had provided didn't take long. I spotted the place first since I'd seen a photo of it. There was nothing unusual about the house — a single-story place with a wide driveway and double garage on the right. The only thing that stood out at all was the privacy hedge along the front, which wasn't unheard of but also wasn't exactly common.

When we got a closer look from the side a bit later, we saw the parking spaces Ms. Abboud's report had shown. From the road, they were completely obscured by the greenery.

By then we were sitting, tucked uncomfortably in the middle of a cluster of trees and bushes, a good two hundred feet from the right side of the house. There were two cars parked in front — we assumed whatever vehicle my dad and the others were using was in the garage — but there was no way we could make out the license plates. That might never matter, but who knew?

"Remind me to pick up some binoculars," I said.

Aki didn't answer but that was because he was chewing one of the granola bars I'd tossed into the backpack. He gave me a thumbs-up though, while he reached in for a pear. I wished I'd suggested we stop and grab some lunch before coming here.

It was a couple of hours later when we decided to abandon our cramped hiding place and return early the next morning. There hadn't been much to observe that afternoon. Cars came and went. People went in and came out.

"There was no pattern in the ages of the people we saw," Aki remarked as we drove back toward Ottawa. "Whatever's going on in that house, it's not something specific to a certain age group."

That hadn't occurred to me, but he was right. There'd been young and old people, mostly adults but not exclusively. A young couple had a small child with them, and one woman had been accompanied by a teen.

"The ones who came and left after we got here all stayed about forty minutes," I said, thinking of Aki's reference to patterns. "Did you notice anything else?"

He hadn't. But I felt sure we'd do better the next day. For one thing, we planned to get there early enough to see my father and the others arrive. I wasn't too hopeful about what we'd learn from that, but it wouldn't hurt to give it a shot.

And more importantly, we'd have binoculars, so we'd be able to see details we hadn't been able to make out today. I got Aki to stop at a sporting goods store and picked up two pairs of a kind the clerk recommended.

Then I almost messed up by paying with a credit card, only stopping myself at the last second. As I paid by debit instead, I tried to remember if either of my parents was on that bank account. I know Mom is on the savings, but this one is for general use. My "official allowance" goes in there and I've never had either of my parents ask me anything about how I spend it. That makes me think my name is the only one on the account, but I can't be one hundred percent sure.

I should probably make a point of going into the bank and asking a few questions.

Meanwhile, the stash of bills in my closet would probably be the best way to pay for things. There was still a fair amount of cash there and as far as I knew, no one else was aware of it.

As the clerk passed the bag with the binoculars over the counter, another surge of anger rippled through me. It was ridiculous, the thought that I had to sneak around and hide things, as if *I* was the one doing something wrong.

But at least I'd found someone to help me. Aki had surprised me when I brought up the matter of payment earlier, as we'd sat scrunched in our hiding place.

"Twenty bucks an hour, plus gas," he'd said.

He could easily have asked for twice that. I obviously needed his help, and he'd been to my house, so he was well aware that my family had money. But I sensed he'd thought it through and decided on an amount he felt was fair.

I was grateful for that since I had no idea how long this was going to take or what else might be needed.

Aki dropped me off a few houses away from mine. He'd understood and agreed it would be best if neither of my parents met him for the time being.

"I'll meet you right here in the morning. Six thirty," I said as I swung the door open and stepped out.

As he drove off, it occurred to me that I didn't know anything about him. His life, where he lived, how he usually spent his time. I wondered if he was used to getting up early. I sure wasn't. And the night ahead didn't look too promising.

It's never easy to sleep when things are bad with Nora.

CHAPTER THIRTEEN

I've gotten used to the ups and downs. So now, when Nora breaks up with me, I don't care at first. Sometimes, if we've been squabbling a lot, I'm even glad. Then I make up my mind not to text or call or go see her. In those moments I feel like I'm done with her for good.

It changes though. Even when I try to hang onto my resolve, I can't. Once the anger is gone it leaves room for other things, and I start missing her and wanting things to be okay with us again.

Owen (this won't come as a surprise) says I'm a sucker for punishment. Which led, the last time this happened, to me claiming I would *not* give in first if she dumped me again. I can even hear the echo of my own words.

"You're right, I *do* have to stop letting her walk all over me. If she does this again, I swear I'll wait it out as long as it takes."

"And if she doesn't make a move?" Owen had asked skeptically.

"Then that will be that."

I checked my phone a record number of times early in the evening, but I knew very well there'd be no text from her. Especially not this soon.

Eventually, I felt guilty and forced myself to cross the room and put it, face down, on a shelf. Mom and I were watching the first episodes of a series she'd come across and thought we'd both enjoy. It was good, a crime thriller stretched out over half a dozen episodes, and I shouldn't have let myself get distracted. I knew she'd noticed but she hadn't said anything, yet.

"Sorry," I said, sliding back into my seat. "I didn't mean to be rude."

Mom lifted the remote and pressed pause.

"Is there anything you want to talk about?" she asked.

"Not really. But thanks."

"Then I guess I can assume it's Nora."

"Yeah. But it's no big deal," I said.

For a second I thought she was going to say something else, but she let it drop, sighed, and switched the show back on.

Later, as I was lying in bed thinking about things, I felt a small surge of satisfaction that I hadn't sent so much as a single word to Nora, though there'd been a few tempting moments.

On the way to what Aki had taken to calling "the location" the next morning I remembered to suggest we grab some breakfast first. He didn't argue, and he didn't protest when I insisted on paying.

"It's part of your expenses," I said. "And it could be a long morning, so we'd better get some muffins or whatever for later on too."

Even with the delay we were tucked in (and full!) almost an hour before the sedan pulled into the driveway.

"Arrival time, twenty minutes to eight," Aki said.

He was leaning forward, as much as he could in our cramped space, and I realized he'd pulled a flip pad out of his pocket and was jotting that detail down.

I lifted my binoculars and got them focused on the car just as the garage door slid open. It was just starting to close again when two figures emerged from the car. My father and the car's driver both got out of the front. The back door on the passenger side had begun to open as well by the time our line of vision was cut off, so I knew there was at least one more person inside.

As I lowered my binoculars, I saw that Aki had been using his too. As soon as he set them down, he began making another note on his pad. I leaned over a bit and saw it was a license plate number.

"Great thinking!" I told him. "You sure this is your first spy job?"

"I can't divulge that kind of sensitive information," he answered, deadpan.

It was just after eight when two other cars drove into the outside parking places. The first carried an older couple while the second car brought a couple, I'd say in their mid-twenties. She was obviously pregnant.

"She's helping him walk," Aki observed as the younger couple made their way to the door.

I looked more carefully and saw that he was right. You'd have thought it would be the other way around, but she was definitely helping support him, with one hand under his elbow.

"He's limping a little," I pointed out.

That was about the most interesting thing we saw while we were there. People came and went. Nothing remarkable happened. No pattern emerged. We got the license numbers from most of the vehicles, but what we might ever do with them neither one of us could imagine.

Around nine-thirty, we ate the muffins and each drank a bottle of juice. We'd realized early on that we needed to be careful about drinking too much. Not that there wasn't plenty of cover behind us to take a leak in, but it was still a risk. If someone opened the door while we were moving, it was possible they'd notice something.

"I don't think there's much point in sitting here any longer today," I said.

"You're probably right," Aki agreed. "Anything else you want to check out?"

"What about this," I said. "What about if we go back to the car around the time someone should be coming out, and see if we can follow them?"

"Let's do it," he said. "There's an older couple who should be leaving next. Let's get back to the car and get in position."

We kept low, bent over and walking carefully so we weren't leaving a noticeable trail of broken branches or trampled grass as we moved through the trees toward the car. Aki had located a near perfect place to park when we were here yesterday. He'd turned off the road at what looked like the end of a gravel driveway and headed into the edge of a wooded field. The trees there were sparse enough to maneuver through, but thick enough to effectively hide the car once he'd driven in a little way.

I'd wondered how difficult it would be when it came time to leave. The idea of backing the car out the way it had been driven in seemed impossible, but he was able to turn around by making short back and forward turns.

Luckily, there were no houses across from that field. That would have raised our odds of being seen when we were driving in or out. Of course, there was always a chance that someone driving by would notice us. But unlike a homeowner, who might call the police to check up on us, a motorist would probably wonder for a second or two what we were doing there and then forget all about it.

Best of all, our secret parking place was less than a five-minute walk from "the location," even though we were moving at a slow, stealthy pace.

We'd just made it back out to the road when the old couple's red SUV pulled out. It turned south, away from us. Aki pulled out onto the road and began following it. The driver was maintaining a speed below the limit, so we did too. Other vehicles grabbed the first chance they got to pass us, and then did the same with the old couple, which we figured worked in our favor. If the old fellow happened to be glancing in his rearview mirror with any regularity, he'd see a variety of cars. No reason to notice ours.

That seemed improbable though. No one we'd seen at "the location" had shown the least concern that anyone could be watching. There were no furtive glances around or efforts to hide their faces. I mentioned this fact to Aki.

"Could be because everything is on the up and up," he said.

"Or the people going there *think* it is, anyway," I said.

Aki shot a quick look at me.

"As in, they're being conned in some way?" he asked.

"I guess. I mean, what else fits with my father pretending to be other places on business when he's right here?"

"Maybe he's doing something legit that has to be kept secret," Aki said.

I wondered if he actually believed that might be true. And why it hadn't even crossed my mind.

"Too bad we can't get a look into the place from the back yard," I said. "We might be able to figure out what's going on if we could see inside."

"I wonder how late they stay," Aki said. "If it was getting dark, and we had on clothes that blended in, maybe —"

"I doubt they're still at it that late," I said. "And there's not a bit of cover back there. Nothing but a few spindly trees a squirrel couldn't hide behind."

The couple we were following had reached the city by then. They turned north and Aki did the same. Before long they exited into the Carlington neighborhood and shortly after that they pulled into the driveway of an older style brick house.

The man got out first and went around to open the passenger door and help the woman, whom I took to be his wife, out. She smiled up at him and he patted her hand with his. That was all we saw before Aki drove past.

We got a second look a moment later when we drove by again on our way out of the subdivision.

"If these people are marks of some kind," Aki commented, "I wonder what a scammer could get from them."

I got his point, of course. This residential area is nice, but it isn't an area where you'd expect to find any great wealth.

"What was your general impression of the people we saw coming and going today and yesterday?" I asked.

"You mean, did they look well off?"

"Yeah."

"Not really. I wasn't looking for that, though. But no, I think we'd have noticed if everyone was driving high-end vehicles and dressed expensively."

"It's not like we could see the labels on their clothes," I pointed out.

"True. But think about it, Ethan. There's a difference in the way people move when they're walking around with designer clothes and bags."

He was right. And I was suddenly uncomfortable about the brand names I was wearing. I wondered if there was something in my walk, a confident assurance that wasn't there when the Granger family had been living on a lower income.

And do other people look at us with envy, or admiration, or resentment, or what? How do people with less feel about people with more?

Life is sure easier now than it used to be. No sense pretending it isn't.

"Ethan?"

I realized Aki had asked me something, but I'd missed it, off in my own thoughts.

"Sorry, man. What did you say?"

"I was asking if you want to go back to the location for a while."

"Uh, I can't. I told Owen I'd go to the gym with him this afternoon. But you do whatever you like. I mean, if you want to go back that's great but don't feel like you have to."

"Okay. I'll let you know later on what I decided."

I got Aki to drop me off at Owen's place. The note I'd left for Mom on the counter had said, "I'll be at Owen's" so this more or less made it true. I'd basically overcome any guilt I felt about lying to Dad when I needed to, but Mom was a different story.

Owen knew my plan for the morning, so he was expecting me. He was also raring to get to the gym.

Kylie was working again, and she greeted us with a friendly smile. But then she turned to Owen and said, "I see you brought your own trainer again today."

He laughed. "Yeah. He's my biggest inspiration."

I didn't find it quite as amusing as they did, although I think I hid my annoyance as I told Owen I was going to warm up on the treadmill. A moment later Kylie appeared at my side.

"Sorry if I crossed the line back there."

"What? Nah, that was nothing."

"You sure? I never mean any harm but sometimes my humor comes across the wrong way."

"Forget it," I said, and gave her a smile. Then I lowered my voice, tried to look menacing, and added, "But don't ever do it again."

She looked startled for a second. Then she laughed and headed toward a customer coming in the door.

Owen had a different trainer this time and this guy pushed him harder than Rohan had. He was flushed and sweating as he headed for the showers and when he emerged, he hesitated before booking his next workout.

On the way home he confirmed my suspicion as to why he'd suddenly gotten interested in getting fit.

"I hope it's going to be worth it," he said.

"Like, building strength and stamina?"

"Right. And maybe bringing my single status to an end."

"Good," I said. "It's about time."

Owen just nodded at that.

"Anyone I know?" I asked.

"Actually," he said, drawing the word out and giving me a sideways glance, "she's a friend of Nora's."

"Which one?"

"Bahiriya Osmani."

It took me a few seconds to answer and when I did all I could get out was, "Wow."

Don't get me wrong, Owen is a great guy. He's likeable, quick-witted, and has all kinds of good qualities. But Bahiriya —man, she stands out! She's one of those people who practically shines, the way she's so friendly and gracious and funny. Oh yeah, and gorgeous. Plus, really smart. She won some kind of science award back a year or two ago. I don't remember what it was about exactly, but I have a vague idea it was a green initiative.

There was nothing strange about Owen being interested in Bahiriya. I mean, who wouldn't be! But if he thought he had a shot, if he actually meant to make a move for her, well, I didn't see that ending well.

"You think Nora might be willing to help? Put in a good word for me, or maybe even have a small party?"

I'd have thought he was kidding if he hadn't looked so hopeful. Nora is about as fond of Owen as he is of her. I think I've made that pretty clear already. What's more, he knew it. His judgment must have been totally skewed by this new infatuation.

But at least I had an out.

"Nora and I broke up," I said.

"What? *Now*?" He looked outraged at the idea that I'd gotten dumped just at a time when he wanted my girlfriend to do something for him.

"Afraid so," I said.

"That girl is so annoying," Owen remarked, like he hadn't just been suggesting she act as an unofficial assistant in his quest for love.

"I'm okay though," I said.

If that had been a bid for sympathy (it wasn't) Owen would have missed it completely.

"Yeah, great, but how long do you think this will last?"

"What? The breakup?"

"Yes."

"Far as I know, this is it. The actual end. Unless she makes a move, which has never happened."

"Well, I know that, but you always —"

His words trailed off and I knew he was remembering how he'd made me swear I wouldn't do my usual thing of trying to make up with Nora if she broke up with me again. Which, obviously, she had just done.

CHAPTER FOURTEEN

It was comical, in a mean sort of way, watching Owen process what was happening.

After all, he'd been the one pressuring me to ditch Nora for practically the whole time I'd been going out with her. Or, barring that, to "quit being a complete wuss" whenever she said it was over.

Except, of course, now he wanted me back with her, for his own agenda, and here I was, sticking to my guns.

The truth was, I'd been on the verge of texting her a bunch of times. The only thing that stopped me was how tied up I'd been with other things.

Like spying on my father.

"Well, anyway, you guys always make up eventually," he said at last.

"I dunno about this time," I said. It was probably wrong that I was enjoying the slightly desperate expression on his face. "I guess we just have to wait to see what she does when I don't make the first move."

"I guess," Owen said sadly.

"You want to know how things went this morning?"

"With you and your hired spy? Sure."

"Let's grab a coffee first. I'm parched."

We walked half a block up the street from the gym to where a combination bakery and coffee shop was situated. Once we were at a table with coffee and a couple of raspberry strudels (at Owen's insistence that it would be rude to ignore the bakery side of things) I gave him a quick rundown.

"So, you sat in a bush and followed some random old people," Owen summarized.

I ignored that.

"I wish we could get inside the place. Without that I don't know how we're going to figure out what's going on."

"Maybe you can hire a burglar," Owen suggested with a smirk. "Or see if your spy wants to expand his resumé to add breaking and entering."

"If the back field wasn't so wide open, we could probably get a look through one of the windows, which might tell us something."

"There's nowhere to hide there at all?"

"Nope. The only side with cover is the one we're using. That faces a solid wall with one small window, which looks into the garage."

"Is the garage locked?"

"Probably. We haven't risked trying to get in there — all we'd see would be the car anyway."

But as I was saying that an idea struck me.

"A drone!" I blurted. "We might be able to get some shots inside with a drone!"

"They'd hear it. Or see it."

"You're right."

My shoulders slumped. It was so frustrating, being on the outside with no way to see what was going on in that place. Something where people of all different ages and, by what Aki and I had seen, varying financial situations, were going for about half an hour at a time.

"Wait!" I said. "There are some saplings on the lawn behind the house. Maybe we could mount cameras there, pointed toward the windows. Wireless cameras we could turn off and on with a remote!"

"So, actually mounted there, on their property, to record what's happening inside?" Owen said.

"Yes! Do you think it would work?"

"I think it would be illegal is what I think. I mean, if your aim is to get a criminal record you could be on to something, but if not, you need to keep thinking."

"As if my own father would press charges," I said.

"Your father isn't doing whatever he's up to alone, though, is he? Who knows what the other guys might do."

"Yeah, but —"

"But nothing. You have no idea what you're messing with here, bro. You can't assume *anything*. This could be dangerous."

I had no answer for that. Which is my typical reaction when I'd *like* to argue but I think he's probably right.

By that time, we'd eaten the pastries and drained our cups. Most of the shop's customers were getting things to go, but it still seemed wrong to monopolize a table when there were only a few of them. We took our cups to the counter, Owen told the woman at the cash register the strudel was amazing, and we called for a ride home.

I went to his place for a bit, but it wasn't a great day. Phil was on edge, and Owen's mother was giving him a hard time one minute and trying to kiss up to him the next. It was easy to see Owen was embarrassed, even though I've witnessed similar performances lots of times. He looked relieved when I left.

I almost texted Nora that evening. The phone was in my hand, and I was composing what I wanted to say in my head. Or trying to. It couldn't be a message about getting back together, or claiming I was sorry for whatever had provoked her. Because, for the first time, I was determined not to, as Owen put it, "crawl back to her."

And that was a problem — trying to think of something to say that wasn't one of those two things, but that would lead into a conversation about patching things up between us. I really hate it when we're split up, even though it's not scary like it used to be.

It got me wondering how many times she'd dumped me before I got so used to it that I more or less assumed we'd get back together. It had to be at least half a dozen. And how many since then?

I don't get all that upset anymore. Now it's basically a sort of unsettled, slightly anxious feeling, waiting for things to right themselves. Which doesn't sound like anything much, but it's not something I enjoy either.

I just wish things could go along smoothly, like they do for some couples. Owen and his ex were like that. Not that they never argued, but when they did, that's all it was.

A text alert startled me as I was thinking about all this. Could it be Nora, reaching out to me for a change?

Nope. It was Aki. And he had something interesting to tell me. Could I meet him at the corner where we'd been connecting? He'd be there in a couple of minutes, and it shouldn't take long. Half an hour should be plenty.

I was already stepping into my shoes as I let him know I was on my way. By the time I reached the corner he was there, waiting.

He spoke as soon as I was in the passenger seat with the door closed.

"I feel a bit foolish for getting you to meet about this. It really isn't much at all."

"If it's more than what we've found out so far, then it's something," I said as Aki pulled the car away from the curb and drove slowly up the street. "Besides, you never know what could turn out to be important."

"Okay, so I went back late this afternoon," he said. "Mainly to find out what time they wrap up, in case that matters. And while I was there, watching the usual movement — people coming and going, the door on the side of the garage opened and one of the men came out."

"Was it my dad?" I blurted.

"I don't know what your dad looks like," he said.

"Oh. Right."

"But I got a picture," he added.

With that, he passed his phone to me so I could take a look for myself.

The photo was from a distance and had clearly been taken in haste. Which was understandable since he wouldn't have known how long he had to get it. It showed a man from the side, looking out over the back field.

"Is this your father?"

"No. But I think it could be one of the men I saw with him that first day." My eyes moved from the face to his body. "What's he wearing anyway?"

"That's what I mainly wanted to tell you. It looks like a lab coat."

"A lab coat," I repeated. "That's weird."

"It has to mean something though. About what they're doing there. Some kind of scientific experiment or maybe even medical testing."

"Well, I can tell you this for sure, my dad has no background whatsoever in anything like that, or anything else that would need a lab coat."

"He might be in charge, or have some other role, like, if they're — I don't know, working on something secret maybe."

That seemed like a stretch. Something out of a movie. But still, I thought about it for a minute before answering.

"I mean, I can't see it. At all. But I guess it's not *impossible.* Except, what about all the people we saw going in and out?"

"They could be part of a test group of some sort. Clinical trials, maybe," Aki said. "So, whatever your father is doing could be one hundred percent legit, but he's not allowed to tell anyone."

Did I ever want to believe that. Even though I'd never heard my father suggest he knew, or cared, anything about scientific studies or medical experiments, I really hoped Aki was right.

"We need to find out more," I said.

"I agree, but this is a start at least," Aki said. "So, what next?"

"He's supposed to be home tomorrow, sometime in the afternoon," I said. "Let's go out mid-morning. With any luck we can find out where they go when they leave. That might help."

"Sure. No problem."

"Perfect. I'll meet you at the corner at ten. And, by the way," I said, nodding at the image on his phone, "great job on getting this."

Aki smiled. "You want to send it to yourself, to look at again later?" he asked.

"You know what — I'd better not. At this point I don't know what my father has access to on my devices."

"Including your phone?"

"Especially my phone." I couldn't even explain how nervous that made me, but when it had occurred to me earlier, I'd taken a quick look through recent exchanges and activities. Luckily, Aki and I had only exchanged a few texts and there was nothing specific enough to raise suspicions. We agreed to text as little as possible, and to be careful to keep messages vague.

And then he said something that sent a chill all through me.

"You might want to disable your location tracking, just in case."

CHAPTER FIFTEEN

I was exhausted when Aki picked me up on Monday morning. Apparently, it showed.

"You look like a victim from some gruesome horror story," Aki remarked.

I laughed. "Thanks," I said. "I couldn't get to sleep last night."

"I hear that."

Except for a drive-through order, that summed up our conversation until we got out to "the location" and settled into our usual hiding place. Feeling the way I did, I was hoping we wouldn't be there long. It turned out to be over three hours though, before we finally saw signs that they might be wrapping things up. Of the people who'd come and gone that morning, the last two cars had left about fifteen minutes apart. The parking places sat empty.

"I hope they're not just breaking for lunch," Aki said.

They weren't. Just a few minutes later, the garage door slid up and the sedan backed out, turned, and headed for the road.

The second it was out of sight, we hightailed it for Aki's car. It only took a few minutes since there was no need for stealth.

There was no hurrying the next part though, since he had to be careful maneuvering his way out with the car. By the time we reached the road, the sedan was nowhere to be seen.

"Left or right?" he asked.

"Try left," I said. It seemed most likely, assuming they were heading back to the city.

Even so, we were both on edge until we neared the first intersection and saw the sedan stopped there. It was signaling to turn right, and Aki followed at a distance until we got closer to the city and traffic got heavier. Then it got a bit challenging to keep up but there was less chance of being noticed. And Aki managed not to lose them although it was close a couple of times.

The sedan ended up dropping my dad and the other two men off in behind the strip mall where I'd first seen them. Aki drove into the parking lot in front, and I slid down in my seat to where I wouldn't be noticeable but could still see what was going on. It didn't take long before two vehicles pulled out and drove away.

My dad's wasn't one of them. Which I found strange. My father isn't the kind of guy to sit around wasting time and I couldn't think of what he might be doing back there, alone in his vehicle.

A moment or two later though, the reason for his delay became clear. A small white car pulled in off the street and drove up and in behind the strip mall.

"That could be the car Ms. Abboud photographed," I whispered, as if they might hear me. That made me laugh. Nervous tension, probably.

"I'll see if I can get a shot of it when it comes back out," Aki said. He slipped his phone out of his pocket and put it up like he was talking into it. I stayed down while he clicked a half a dozen times.

"Don't move yet," he cautioned a few seconds later. "Your dad's vehicle is pulling out now too."

When it was safe to sit back up Aki passed me his phone so I could swipe the photos of the white car. The first couple of shots were disappointing. A small white car that looked like a gazillion other small white cars. But on the third photo I felt my heart begin to hammer like crazy.

"It can't be," I said, staring at the driver, who'd come into focus as the car went by.

"What is it?" Aki asked.

"I know this woman. The driver," I told him.

"Seriously? Who is it?"

I hesitated, which Aki picked up on right away.

"No need to tell me if you'd rather not," he said quickly.

That made me feel bad. Did he think I didn't trust him all of a sudden?

"It's Nora's mother," I said.

Aki whistled, long and low. Then we sat saying nothing for a couple of minutes. I was trying to process what I was looking at and I can only imagine what jumble of thoughts might be going through his head.

"I don't know what to make of this," I said at last. "But it's probably time to call it a day anyway." A night of restless sleep, hours watching the place, and then the shock of what I'd just seen made me feel like heading to my spot by the Gatineau and letting my eyes close. And that's what I'd have done if another urge wasn't suddenly even more insistent.

Nora. Now being quite certain her mother was connected to what was going on made me want to protect her. That sounds a bit nuts, I know. But at the moment, going to her was the only thing I could think about.

I paid Aki what he'd earned so far, added enough to be sure his gas was covered, and gave him an address to drop me off at. When I stepped out of his car, I was on the next block over from Nora's place.

Even before Aki's car was out of sight, I regretted it. What was I doing there? I had no plan, nothing except the vague thought that I might run into Norah's mom and ... then what?

What did I hope to accomplish, besides looking weak and pathetic? It wasn't like her mom was going to rush out and tell me she'd just seen my dad and explain what that was about.

The more likely scenario was that *Nora* would see me. If that happened, she'd be in there snickering to herself, smug and triumphant in the thought that I couldn't hold out.

So, I took a deep breath and found the resolve to turn and walk the other way. A decision that almost got me killed.

Even now, I'm not quite sure how it happened. Yes, I was definitely distracted, thinking about all the stuff going on with my dad, the situation with Nora, and the fact that the woman in the photo driving that white car was her mother. But it wasn't as though I stepped into the street without looking. That's so automatic, a glance left and right. I saw nothing.

Yet, somehow, there *was* a car, and it was heading straight toward me. I heard a squeal of brakes but had no time to react before it slammed against me and hurled me through the air.

I'm not sure if I was knocked out or just stunned by the impact with the pavement. Nor do I know how long I was suspended in whatever state it was, but I can say for sure everything was weirdly silent and distant.

Then it was all back in a rush. Voices yelling, running footsteps, someone wailing, questions.

I realized after a bit that the questions were directed at me.

"Can you hear me?" "Are you all right?" "Can you move?"

I heard the questions, but I couldn't sort out what to answer first, if, that is, I could manage to speak.

A man approached, asked everyone to step back, said he knew what to do, and knelt beside me. He checked my breathing and talked to me. He told me help was on the way and said I was doing fine. He asked my name, and I did my best to tell him, but my best sounded like someone talking with a mouthful of marbles.

"Okay, don't worry about talking," he said. "Can you hold up one finger for yes, and two for no?"

With some effort, I lifted an index finger.

"And to signal no?"

I managed to raise two fingers.

"That's great," he said. "Now I'm going to see if you have a phone on you, okay?"

I gave him a "yes" signal and felt him reaching into my pockets and pulling out my phone.

He didn't have the passcode, of course, but that didn't matter. I'd used it recently enough that it wasn't locked.

"Okay, so you're Ethan Granger?" he asked, and nodded when I confirmed.

"And my name is Jayamma Chidozie," he said. "I'm going to look in your contact list for a parent. All right? Good."

It was then that a loud, almost angry voice rose in the background.

"The kid came out of nowhere. Walked right in front of me. There was no way I could get stopped in time."

"Sir," Jayamma said, "can you put a pin in that for now?"

"I'm just saying, this was *not* my fault. I mean, I hope the kid's okay, but I'm not responsible."

Jayamma ignored that. He asked if he could call one of my parents. I think I signaled him to go ahead, but I'm not sure. My thoughts were starting to swim, and I felt a chill creeping over me.

And then the ambulance arrived. They put something around my neck, moved me to a stretcher, and put a blanket over me up to my shoulders.

I vaguely remember hearing the siren and taking a minute or two to connect it to the vehicle transporting me to the hospital. At emergency, I was wheeled inside and almost immediately seen to by a doctor.

The doctor examined me and performed a jumble of tests. I remember she shone a light in my eyes and asked me some really easy questions. She asked me about pain but, surprisingly, nothing seemed to hurt too much.

When the doctor was finished, a nurse came and sat with me. She said to be sure to let her know if I felt like I might need to vomit. Also, she seemed to like checking blood pressure, since she took mine what seemed like every few minutes.

After a while the doctor came back, but she wasn't alone. My parents were right behind her.

"Ethan!" Mom said, rushing to my side and promptly bursting into tears.

"Now, Paulette," my father said. "Didn't the doctor just tell us he's going to be fine?"

"The prognosis looks optimistic at this time," the doctor said. "However, we'll need to keep Ethan for at least a day or two to monitor how things go."

"I feel okay," I said.

"And that's a positive sign," said the doctor. "But in cases like this we want to watch for symptoms pointing to concussion."

"Couldn't that be done at home?" Mom asked. "We can certainly hire a nurse."

"There are other potential concerns," the doctor said. "Believe me, it's best for Ethan to be here."

There were no more objections.

Once the doctor had finished explaining everything they'd be doing, Mom settled into the chair next to me and held my hand. The nurse noticed and gave me a smile. I rolled my eyes, just a little, to signal my embarrassment, which was a mistake.

Mom was on her feet in a flash. She gave the nurse a frantic look and cried, "Get the doctor! His eyes are rolling back in his head!"

The nurse stepped closer and peered down at me. "It doesn't look like anything serious is going on," she said. "I'm a trauma nurse. I know what to watch for."

Mom looked doubtful. I could almost see the wheels turning, and I knew she was going to come up with some kind of excuse to call the doctor back in anyway.

"It's okay, Mom," I said. "I was just messing around."

"You were what?"

"I mean, I was sort of checking — to see if I could look up," I said. I knew it sounded lame, but Mom sank back into the chair. This time she grabbed my hand with both of hers.

"Well, you gave me a fright," she said.

I apologized and waited a couple of minutes before extracting my hand. A while later, having noticed my father was starting to pace a little, I commented that it might be less stressful if

I could just rest without anyone there watching me.

Dad jumped on that like a pouncing cat. Within a couple of minutes they were out the door, promising to check on me later.

There was a fair amount of checking on me over the next two days. Mom came by several times each day for short visits, always with supplies from home. Clothes and slippers, toiletries and fruit, books and playing cards, and I can't remember what else, but I know it was enough to fill a medium-sized suitcase (which she also brought) when I was discharged.

Dad stopped by separately the next day. His visit wasn't long either, but we got onto the subject of places we'd been on past vacations. It was a good conversation, with no sign that he was getting bored.

Just before Dad left, a tall black man stepped just inside the doorway.

"Uh, who were you looking for?" Dad asked.

"Ethan Granger." The man looked over at the bed and his face lit up with a smile. "Hey, buddy. Good to see you're doing okay."

It took me a second. "You're the guy who helped me at the scene!" I said. A warm feeling spread through me remembering how his presence had calmed and steadied me.

"What?" my dad said. "Are you Mr. Chidozie?"

"Jayamma, please."

"Stuart," Dad said, extending his hand. "We spoke on the phone that day. My wife and I are so grateful for what you did for our son."

"It was a privilege to be able to help," Jayamma said.

"Naturally, we'd like to give you something," Dad said. "To show our appreciation."

"No, sir," Jayamma said. He looked uncomfortable. "I thank you for the offer, but I cannot accept."

"I understand," Dad said. Before he left, he got Jayamma's contact information, insisting that my mom would want to meet him, and that at the very least they'd like to have him over for a meal.

"Now *that* would be very nice," Jayamma said.

Jayamma didn't stay long. He was on his way to work and said he'd just wanted to see how I was.

"I'll see you when you come for dinner," I told him as he was leaving. "And be warned — my mom will cook enough food for ten people."

He laughed and said, "I'm always up for a challenge."

His visit made me feel so good.

That was also true when Owen dropped in to "see if I was going to make it." He brought me a large Snickers bar, plunked down in the visitor's chair, and promptly fell asleep. When he woke up, he apologized for his "accidental nap," told me to pay attention where I was going next time, and said he'd see me when I got home. If I had to pick a favorite visit, I'd have to say it was his.

I was pleasantly surprised when Aki showed up. His boyfriend, Jean-Guy, was with him. I hadn't met him in person before, although Aki had talked about him a fair amount while we were doing surveillance.

"I told him he should bring something. At least a card," Jean-Guy said.

Aki laughed. "Jean-Guy was scandalized I would visit someone in the hospital empty-handed."

"It's making me re-evaluate our whole relationship," Jean-Guy said.

That make me laugh, which hurt but was worth it.

So, yeah. I had my share of visitors, which cheered me up and helped pass the time. But there was one person I kept hoping might walk through the door.

Nora.

She never came.

CHAPTER SIXTEEN

When I was discharged from the hospital, it was with a diagnosis of a concussion, which I convinced myself I'd shake off in a few days. I didn't. It was weeks before I felt halfway decent, and I still wasn't a hundred percent.

No big deal, except for two things.

The first one wasn't exactly disappointing because I didn't know about it ahead of time. Dad had planned this amazing surprise and booked a trip to Machu Picchu so I could ride the Inca Trail in August, instead of waiting until December as originally planned.

He looked so sad telling me about it. Not because he was all that keen to go — it's the kind of thing he'd do just for my sake, but mainly because he knew, under normal circumstances, I'd have been thrilled.

But, of course, taking on that trail this soon was obviously out of the question for someone recovering from a concussion.

Don't think I didn't wrestle with some real guilt, and questions about what I was doing with the spying and whatnot. There were times I almost convinced myself I had to be dead wrong.

Obviously, my father couldn't be a great dad and at the same time be involved in anything seriously bad.

The second thing, which I shouldn't complain about even though it got to be pretty bothersome, was the home nursing I got from Mom.

I can't prove it, but I think Owen found it entertaining the way she fussed over me. Maybe I'm wrong, but it seemed suspicious the way he'd ask me things in a louder voice than usual, and always when Mom was within earshot.

For example:

"Did something hurt? I thought you winced."

"Whoa! Are you dizzy or what?"

At one point I called him on it. He tried to look hurt, like I was accusing him of some terrible crime when all he'd done was try to make sure I was okay. His innocent act, which I'm almost sure was covering an urge to laugh, didn't convince me.

Even so, I dropped it. After all, he was showing up. So what if he made a little sport of the situation? If our roles were reversed, I'd almost definitely do the same thing.

Besides, every time Mom came in to check on one of these false alarms, she asked if we wanted something to eat or drink or whatever, which kept us well stocked up.

A highlight during my recovery was Jayamma's visit. As I'd warned him, Mom spared no effort in putting out a big spread, which he obviously enjoyed. She commented afterward what a lovely man he was, so easy to talk to and so appreciative of the meal.

Aki couldn't come over, of course, but when a full week and a half had passed since the accident, I convinced Mom I probably wouldn't keel over and die if I was out of her sight for a few minutes. And that some fresh air would be good for me.

She relented and agreed I could walk to a nearby mini park, but only if I sat on the bench and rested before returning home. There were other instructions too. I was to walk on the part of the sidewalk farthest from the road. If I felt the slightest bit dizzy, I must sit at once on the nearest safe surface, and text for a drive home.

With these guidelines firmly in mind I set off to a small community park where Aki had agreed to meet me. He'd suggested, when he visited me in hospital, that when I felt up to it, we should re-evaluate our strategy. I had to agree we weren't learning much by hanging around and watching people come and go for hours. With any luck and a bit of tossing ideas around, we should be able to figure out what else we could try.

He was already on the bench when I got there. Jean-Guy was sitting next to him but as I approached, he stood, offered a friendly greeting, and started to walk toward Aki's car, which was parked a short way down the street.

"Jean-Guy and I have plans afterward," Aki said, "so he'll just wait in the car while we talk."

"I don't mind him joining us if he's good with keeping things to himself," I said.

"He's totally trustworthy," Aki said without hesitation.

We called Jean-Guy back, swore him to secrecy, and gave him a rundown of what we were doing and why. I surreptitiously watched his reactions, to see if they looked genuine. They did. When someone's pretending to be shocked or surprised or whatever, you can almost always tell. There's something off in their timing, or overdone in the way they respond.

It confirmed my instincts about trusting Aki. If he hadn't told his boyfriend, then he wasn't telling anyone else either.

"So *that's* what you've been doing on your 'top secret assignment,'" Jean-Guy said. "I thought you were trying to make some dull job sound exciting."

Aki laughed.

"There couldn't *be* a much duller job than stuffing yourself into a bush and staring at a house for hours," he said. "Especially when you're there alone."

"Could I go along? Just to keep you company?"

They both looked at me.

"If that's how you want to spend your free time, sure," I said.

"Any time I spend with this guy is great," Jean-Guy said with a shy smile.

"Tell me that again when you've been crammed between branches for a few hours," I said, but I kind of got the impression he wasn't going to mind all that much.

We got down to the business of thinking up a new plan. After a quick review of our efforts so far, Jean-Guy brought up something I hadn't thought of.

"So, the only time you guys saw them leave was that Monday, when they were wrapping up and heading home?"

"Right."

"What if you try following them on days when they're still in mid-operation. If whatever they're doing always goes on for three or four days, find out where they go at the end of the first couple of days, when they aren't going back to their normal lives."

I liked that idea a lot. And I threw in one I'd had while lying around for days.

"Great suggestion. And I've been thinking that, instead of watching the house for hours in the daytime, we should pick one of their — I don't know what to call them — clients I guess, and follow when they're leaving, like we did with the old couple."

"Yes!" Aki agreed. "There could be a pattern or connection or something that will point us to what's happening there."

"How many license plate numbers do we have so far?" I asked.

"I'd have to check to be exact but it's gotta be a couple dozen or more. There are the ones we got before your accident, and I spent a few hours there each of the three days the men were there last week."

With a new, and hopefully better, plan in place, Aki and Jean-Guy were ready to leave. It was time for me to get back home too, before my mom decided to check up on me. But as the guys were nearing the sidewalk, Aki suddenly turned back by himself.

"I was just wondering," he said quietly when he got close enough, "how everything is going with Nora."

There was an instant lump in my throat, just because he'd bothered to ask.

"I haven't heard a word from Nora since that day you saw her at my place," I said.

"Sorry, man."

"No, you know what, don't be sorry. It's been hard in one way, but I think it's something I needed to find out."

"Are you sure she knows what happened to you? Getting hit by the car?"

"She knows."

I waited then, expecting him to tell me there were loads of other girls out there or some such thing, but he didn't. He nodded and gave my arm a quick squeeze.

"Her loss," he said.

I wondered, as I walked home, whether Nora would ever see it that way. It seemed doubtful, even though there'd been lots of times I'd been sure her feelings for me were as solid as mine for her.

As I'd told Aki, I knew she was aware of the accident. Owen had texted her, as he put it, "under protest" the first day I got back home. There'd been no reply.

There was something about that, something about the fact that I knew *she* knew, and that she'd chosen silence as her response, that helped keep me from reaching out. Even on days I was at my lowest, from the concussion and from thinking about her, I didn't give in.

But it was more complicated than that now. I'd given a lot of thought to what her mother could have been doing, meeting up with my dad that day, and nothing I could come up with seemed innocent. I knew it wasn't a romantic thing at least. (How gross would that have been?) But there was something there, something I couldn't figure out, that tied her into this whole business.

Nora, of course, knew nothing about any of this. But she did know I'd been hurt.

I watched and counted the days as they crept by. The longest we'd stayed broken up in the past was three weeks and two days. It hadn't been like this, though. There'd been lots of exchanges — some full of brokenness, some angry, some hopeful. There'd never been this dead air.

I hated it but I also held onto it. It was over and that was that. Which sounds a lot tougher than I felt, but on the other hand, I was tapping into strength I never thought I had.

And then, on day sixteen, she showed up at my door.

I almost didn't answer the bell. Mom gets a lot of deliveries, and sometimes the delivery person rings or knocks before they see the notice with safe-drop instructions. Usually, by the time I go to check, the package has been dropped and there's no longer anyone there.

But I was bored. So, I ambled my way to the door and pulled it open. And there she was, looking about as gorgeous as I've ever seen her.

"Hi," she said. Her voice was soft and kind of sad.

I reached out and in the next second we were holding onto each other, and I was trying hard not to let tears happen.

"I missed you so much," I said.

"I kept waiting to hear from you," Nora said.

"I didn't think you wanted to," I said.

She leaned back a little, looked up, and shook her head gloomily. "Yeah, but you usually say you're sorry at least. You didn't even do that."

"Well, I'm glad you're here," I said. "And I *am* sorry we had a fight."

She squinted a bit, like she was trying to figure out the answer to a trick question. Probably wondering why I hadn't taken all the blame the way I have in the past.

Maybe it was the concussion. Or maybe it was that she'd shown no interest in how I was doing after the accident, and the fact that there'd been no communication since then either. But I think it was mainly because I honestly couldn't remember what the fight had been about.

I waited, bracing myself for whatever came next.

When she finally spoke again, she said, "Okay, so anyway, I've decided to give you another chance."

I thought about that later. She'd made the first move, showing up at my door. That was good. And we'd patched things up, which I was happy about.

And yet, I felt uneasy.

CHAPTER SEVENTEEN

I was impressed with how Owen stuck with his workout routine. His past history, if the brief and feeble workout attempts he'd made previously could even be called that, hadn't made me think he was suddenly going to turn into a fitness buff.

And yet, here he was, heading to the gym every day or two, and, maybe even more astonishing, jogging! He had his route planned so that he finished at my place, which I appreciated, especially after his little parlor trick of getting Mom to baby me stopped working.

Sometimes he'd flex his biceps and say something like, "Be honest with me, Ethan. Do these guns make you nervous?"

Or, "I tell ya, it's getting harder and harder to fight off the ladies."

"I thought the whole idea was to *get* their attention," I reminded him.

"Well, yeah, but just one. Not these Owen-crazed swarms."

I didn't actually see much in the way of muscle mass, but I knew that would come in time if he kept it up. What I *did* see was how it was affecting him in other ways. He was clearly more confident, and happier.

Seeing that helped offset the gloom I'd been struggling against lately. The lingering effects of the concussion, being stuck in the house so much, and of course the whole situation with my dad were all weighing on me.

Even being back together with Nora didn't do much to lift my spirits. I kept wondering how her mom was involved with whatever my dad was up to, and how it was all going to play out. There was no way she and I would survive the fallout of a scandal.

So, while I tried to stay upbeat, it wasn't easy.

And, of course, it was frustrating to feel like Aki and I were making so little progress. Once I'd begun feeling close to normal, I'd counted on us getting somewhere with our new plan, but that wasn't happening.

I could see that Aki was feeling the same way. He started commenting regularly that we needed a break. Not the "take time off" kind of break. A bit of luck.

And then we got one. A big one.

It was a Thursday evening. Dad had "left" the day before after telling me and Mom he'd be a bit longer than usual this time. His "out of town" trips were usually no more than four days, but he predicted he'd be away for five or six this time.

This was the second so-called trip he'd been on since we'd been following the new plan, and while it was a lot less tedious than what we were doing before, we hadn't really learned much.

We already knew the routine Dad and the others followed. They'd finish with whatever appointments they had by around eight p.m. Once the last car left, there was a gap of time where they must have been cleaning up and getting things ready for the next morning. That made sense because people started arriving almost as soon as they got there each day.

The first evening we followed them after they left the place, we discovered that the men spent their nights at another house not far from the one we were watching. Aki and I figured it either belonged to one of the others, or it could be a rental they were using.

We watched it for a while that night. My dad and the other guys went in, and while we could tell some lights were on, all the window coverings were closed so it was impossible to see what they were doing. Eating probably, maybe sitting around talking, doing normal life things, and then turning in. Once all the lights were out on the side of the house we could see, we left.

The same routine was followed the next two nights. Nobody left.

After that, we decided just to watch the place until closing every now and then and only follow them if they went in a different direction. So, it was just lucky we were there that Thursday night.

It had been a hazy kind of day — dark and overcast, threatening rain. Dreary. As usual, we didn't see the men getting into the sedan and were only alerted that they were leaving by the garage door rising. Then the car backed out.

The driver always reversed into the lot where their clients parked before pulling forward out the lane to the main road.

We were watching them go, ready to sprint back to Aki's car and follow if they happened to drive off in a different direction than usual. But as I got to my feet something caught my eye.

"Aki! Look!"

He turned to where I was pointing and saw what I'd just noticed. The garage door hadn't closed all the way.

"Should we —" he asked.

"We might never get another chance like this," I said, trying to sound more certain than I felt.

"Would we be breaking and entering?"

"I don't know."

"It *is* open," he said.

"So, we're not breaking in. I mean, we could be going in to let someone know the door didn't close."

Aki gave me a look. I probably don't need to describe it.

"Anyway, there'll definitely be a lock on the door to get into the house, so all we'll be able to do is look around the garage."

"What about the security cameras?"

"That's why we've been driving around with the hats and stuff, remember?" I said. But he still looked uneasy.

"You know what, there's no reason for both of us to go in," I said. "I'll do it."

Aki still looked doubtful when we reached his car. I rummaged through the bag of "disguises," dug out a wild-colored shirt from the thrift store, and pulled it on. Then I slapped a wide-brimmed baseball cap on my head.

"Don't forget to keep your head down," he said.

I gave him a thumbs-up, and started back through the trees toward the house. But before I reached the clearing, I heard someone behind me and when I looked, there was Aki. He was wearing a shamrock green sweatshirt that said "Play the Jam," whatever that meant. It had a hood, which he'd arranged to jut out over his forehead.

"You sure?" I asked.

"Yeah. I don't wanna miss out on this after all those hours watching," he said. "Besides, if we get caught, your dad will make sure we don't get in any serious trouble, right?"

I could only tell him I hoped that was true.

Except, in my case, my biggest worry wasn't getting in trouble with the authorities. I was much more afraid of my father catching me spying on him, and having that hanging between the two of us forever. Especially if it happened before I learned anything concrete.

I pushed that thought aside. As we reached the edge of the trees, we paused, looked, and listened carefully to be sure no one was about to drive by. Then we dashed to the garage, threw ourselves down and rolled inside.

My heart was pounding like crazy.

"What if they come back?" Aki whispered, which didn't help calm me any.

"No reason they would," I said back, keeping my voice as quiet as possible. "If they realized the door didn't shut, they'd have stopped and taken care of it right away."

"True," he said. But he had another question. "How do we know for sure there's no one inside?"

I thought, but didn't say, that these might have been good questions to ask before now. And it was an unnerving thought all right. Just because we hadn't seen anyone else, didn't guarantee there wasn't a fourth person involved, someone whose role was to stay on-site full time.

We moved instinctively to the side of the garage against the house and listened for any sound of movement inside. It was quiet, but that didn't exactly prove no one was in there.

"Doesn't matter anyway," Aki said. "There's obviously nothing in here that's going to be helpful."

That was a bit of an understatement. The garage was so bare you'd have thought the property was vacant.

Then I noticed something. The lock on the door into the house was a keypad.

"Too bad we have no way of finding out for sure if anyone's in there," I said. "Because if we knew, I might be able to get us inside."

"Let's knock," Aki suggested. "If anyone answers, we'll say we were out jogging and noticed the door didn't close right."

I thought that would seem lame — and therefore suspicious, but since I had nothing better, I agreed. We knocked good and hard, waited, knocked again and were met with more silence.

Aki looked at me. He raised an eyebrow.

"Okay, so turn around," I said.

He did, and I poked in the numbers in the sequence that would be the next rotation in Dad's system. Nothing except for the tiny red light that indicated a fail. Maybe he didn't use those numbers here, or maybe one of the other guys had picked a code. Still, I wasn't ready to give up. I went on to the fourth possible combination. Nope. And then the fifth.

The light immediately flashed green, and a whirring sound told me it was a go. I turned the handle and swung the door open.

"No way!" Aki said. He forgot to whisper, which made him slam his hand over his mouth so hard it almost knocked him off balance. We barely kept from laughing.

It probably didn't matter anyway. We knew the place had security cameras, but there was only a small chance it was wired for sound. Still, why risk it?

I took a slow, deep breath and stepped inside with Aki right behind me. For a couple of seconds we were frozen in place, staring. Then we looked at each other.

"What the —" Aki said. He remembered to keep his voice down that time.

"This is so weird," I said.

I suppose, if you're staring at a house for hours at a time over a period of a lot of days, what you expect to see when you enter is the inside of a house. Kitchen, living room, bedrooms, bathrooms. So, it was a jolt to find ourselves looking at a room that clearly served as a reception area for anyone coming in the front door. A desk, swivel chair, and a filing cabinet were one side of the room, facing a few chairs on the other.

We checked the filing cabinet. It was locked, which was no surprise. The desk was open but had nothing but blank pads and a few pens. A door on the side of the room opened to a short hall, which is where we went next. Straight ahead there was another door, at which point the hallway turned to the right.

We tried the door and found it unlocked. It led into a room that stretched the rest of the length of the building.

Three hospital beds were set up in there. Each one had tracks on the ceiling above it for the privacy curtains you see in hospital rooms, although the curtains were all open at the moment, giving us a clear view of the whole setup. Small, fold-down tables were attached to the wall on the right side of each bed while lone visitor chairs sat to the left. And that was pretty much it. In a couple of minutes or less we'd seen everything there was to see in there.

We backtracked to the hall. It led to the back part of the place, where there was an office, two bathrooms, and a small kitchen that obviously served as their lunchroom.

A quick examination of the office gave us nothing. A storage unit on the wall was locked, the desk was locked, and the filing cabinet, while unlocked, must have been for show, since it was completely empty.

The storage in the bathrooms held cleaners and spare toilet paper. Not exactly helpful. We ended our inspection in the kitchen, and the first thing we noticed was that one of the double cupboards had locks where there used to be handles. And the fridge had a padlock affixed making it impossible to open the door.

Aki tugged at the lock hanging there but it held firm.

There were things in that place, all right — things that weren't supposed to be seen. What they might be, we couldn't begin to guess, except to say there was some kind of medical connection.

"What are they hiding?" I wondered out loud.

"They might not be hiding anything," Aki remarked. "They might just be making sure certain things are safeguarded."

And I might have tried to convince myself that could be true, if it hadn't been for a small triangle of paper that caught my eye on our way out.

CHAPTER EIGHTEEN

I sometimes wonder how this whole thing would have played out if I hadn't glanced down at that exact spot at exactly that second in time.

But, of course, I did.

It happened as we were passing through the reception area on our way back to the garage, keeping our heads down as we'd done the whole time we'd been inside. Making sure our faces weren't captured by whatever cameras might be hidden.

And so, because my head was down, my attention was caught by a bit of paper so small it almost didn't register. A corner, a shiny triangle of white, peeking out from under the back corner of the desk.

"Hold on," I said.

Aki stopped and looked back at me just in time to see me crouch down and reach underneath. It was a tight fit because the drawers were in that part of the desk, leaving just a couple of inches space between them and the floor. I stretched my fingers as far as they could reach and managed to guide the paper toward me until I could get a hold of it.

As I picked it up, I could see it was a brochure, the kind that's folded in three. The front panel was facing me, glossy and professional, with the words, "The Wonder Treatment They Don't Want You to Know About."

A cold feeling of revulsion shuddered through me.

"Let's go," I said to Aki. "We can look at this when we're out of here."

Aki nodded. He hadn't seen the brochure, but my reaction had to have told him it wasn't good.

We left the way we'd come in, back through the garage, and out from under the partly open door. Once in the open, we made a quick scoot across the driveway and ran to the cover of the wooded area. Not a word was said between us as we hurried to the car and began the drive back.

When we'd nearly reached the city, I finally made myself admit out loud what I'd just discovered.

"It's a medical scam," I said. "They're conning money out of sick people with some phony miracle cure."

Aki kept his eyes straight ahead. You'd have thought he was a super conscientious driver, focusing on the road, but I knew he was being respectful by not looking at me. No doubt what he'd heard in my voice had already told him plenty.

I can't describe what I was feeling but there was a tidal wave of emotion rushing through me. I was angry — furious actually, and ashamed, disgusted, shocked, and a whole lot more. At some point I realized I was clenching my teeth, and I forced my jaws to relax.

"You want to stop at my place for a while?" Aki asked suddenly. "My mom is working and won't be home until after midnight, so we could just hang out, give you time to think."

Time to think was exactly what I needed. I agreed without hesitation, and we were soon driving through a neighborhood that had once been a familiar part of my world.

As we passed places I'd formerly known so well, it hit me that I hadn't been in this district in years. In fact, it was probably the only part of the city I could say that about.

I don't suppose I had to wonder why. The answer was obvious enough although it made me uncomfortable to admit it, even to myself. As Aki guided his car along the streets there was a growing sense of unease stirring in me.

I used to belong here, but that was in the past. My life now was so different in almost every way.

A random memory flashed through my brain. Playing with rocks and sticks and pieces of broken stuff I couldn't readily identify. Not because I had no toys but because it was natural and interesting to create things back in those days.

There'd been no pool in our yard, no grand house full of expensive furnishings and pricey gadgets. No shoebox full of money I didn't need to spend because pretty much anything I wanted was bought for me.

In a strange way, it felt as though the two lives I'd experienced had happened to two different people.

I pulled myself back from these thoughts as Aki parked his car, carefully maneuvering it to the left side of a driveway that was shared with the unit next door. Home to him was a duplex, a dull yellow brick box, with tired lawns.

Once inside his place, Aki tugged open the fridge and, after a slight hesitation, asked me if I was hungry.

I wasn't. Or, rather, I'd been hungry a little earlier but the pamphlet I'd stuck into my pocket had pretty much killed my appetite.

At the same time, it was a safe bet Aki wanted a snack but might not want to make himself something if I wasn't eating too.

"Actually," I said, "I'd kind of like to order something. What do you feel like?"

"I could handle a sub," he said. "There's a deli just a couple of streets over that beats the chains hands down. And they'll deliver, or I could go pick up an order."

"I'd kind of like us to look at this together," I said, sitting the brochure on the table. "Let's get delivery."

He called an order in and then sat cornerwise from me at the table, read the front flap, and unfolded the brochure so we could look at the inside panels.

It was bad.

It was one of those scams claiming a miracle cure that could work on a long list of medical conditions. Claims were made about "big pharma" wanting to keep this information from people because those companies only care about profits, not patients.

There were a number of testimonials from people they had supposedly helped. A man whose cancer had disappeared, completely mystifying the doctors. A woman whose blood sugar went from uncontrollable to normal. A young person with an autoimmune disorder, now symptom-free. And more, each with a remarkable claim and glowing endorsement.

Aki looked up at me after reading through them.

"Do you think it's possible —"

"That any of this is true? Not a chance."

I flipped the brochure over, which is when we saw the "experts." There were two of them, almost certainly the men I'd seen my dad with that first fateful day. Each had a string of credentials after his name, which seemed to cheer Aki.

"Look!" he said. "It would seem your father is working with experts."

"Except, it's easy to get a so-called degree online," I said. "They aren't worth the paper they're printed on."

"That's true," he said. "I suppose if they had bona fide qualifications, we'd have seen certificates displayed somewhere."

"Yup," I said. "I wonder what they charge for this 'wonder treatment' scam."

"Your dad's picture isn't here," Aki said. "Maybe he's not that involved. Is there any way the other guys could have conned him?"

I let myself consider that for less than a minute. I would have liked to believe it, but I knew it wasn't true. If anything, my father would be the one who put it all together. His name didn't appear anywhere on the pamphlet, but all that meant to me was that he was protecting himself.

The subs arrived and I folded the page and slid it back into my pocket. Then I thought better of it and asked Aki if he could put it somewhere for safekeeping. He paused from attacking his foot-long and promised to take care of it. Before I left, he ran a copy off for me on his printer.

I was glad to have the copy to show Owen the next day. He whistled low and, unlike Aki, didn't attempt to make excuses or whitewash my dad's involvement. He did, however, have a question.

"What are you going to do about it?"

It was like a jolt, hearing him ask that way, like he assumed I had some kind of plan.

"What *can* I do?" I said. "I mean, seriously. Confront him? Tell him it's wrong? He already knows that. It's not like I can stop him."

"Are you sure?"

"About — what, about *stopping* him?" I almost laughed, but Owen's face told me he was serious.

"Dude, he's stealing money from sick people."

"I know that, Owen. You think I don't know that? It disgusts me. But what am I supposed to do?"

Owen's eyes shifted away from me, focused on the floor.

"Yeah, I dunno. It's a tough one all right."

And it wasn't like I hadn't been thinking about it. What my own father was doing, cheating people out of their money. How he could do it, knowing he was taking their money for something that was a complete lie.

A swarm of thoughts and questions buzzed around in my brain that night when I was trying to get to sleep.

Were these people refusing conventional treatments — things that could actually help them, believing they'd found something better? The secrecy of the whole thing — was that because he was ashamed on some level, or was it because what they were doing was actually illegal? You'd think it would be against the law to be making bogus medical claims, but the brochure hadn't said what the treatment was. Maybe there was a line they hadn't crossed.

How much money were they taking from each person they were "treating?" Aki had been recording license numbers for a while by then, so we knew at least some of the people were scheduled for repeat appointments. It had to be extremely lucrative, to be covering the overhead and leaving enough profit to make it worth their while.

I wondered how the profits were divided. Knowing my father, it seemed likely he was paying the "experts" with the phony degrees a set amount and keeping a larger share for himself. But what did that actually amount to? Were we living on money Dad made in his legit business, or were we mainly supported by this disgusting setup?

It was at that point I had the first solid idea about how Nora's mom was involved. Working at a critical care center would put her in contact with an endless stream of people being treated for exactly the kinds of medical issues the brochure claimed to cure. There had to be some kind of arrangement where she was doing something to connect patients with this scam.

Something else that occurred to me was that I was responsible for them meeting each other in the first place. Back when Nora and I hadn't been dating for too long, before things went downhill between us, her folks had spent a couple of evenings at our place.

I tried to remember exactly how that had come about, and vaguely recalled a time when Nora's dad was there to pick her up and got chatting with my father. If I have it right, her folks came over for a barbecue later that week, and then there was a second visit a few weeks later. How my father turned that short acquaintanceship into a chance to recruit Nora's mom I couldn't guess, but it wouldn't be that hard for someone as slick as him. Not if she was open to earning some easy money.

I can't describe my fury as I thought about this. Knowing my father had used my relationship with Nora to build a contact for his sleazy con enraged me more than anything I can remember in my entire life.

It overwhelmed me with disgust.

And it brought to mind Ms. Abboud's words of warning the first time I met with her:

Once you know something, you can't un-know it. Whatever you find out is something you'll have to carry for the rest of your days.

Part of me almost wished I'd just dropped the whole thing then and there.

CHAPTER NINETEEN

Nora happened to be at our place when Dad got home a couple of days later. He gave me a one-armed guy-hug, as he calls them, and greeted her in a friendly way. I did my best to stay cool but it was gross, knowing he'd just come from days of ripping off sick people without the slightest sign he was carrying any guilt.

Nora answered his questions — the usual pointless ones. How are you doing? Enjoying the summer break from school? How are your folks? That sort of thing.

Of course, Nora was oblivious to the jeopardy he was putting her mother in. But *I* knew, and *he* knew he was doing something that could hurt her mom and therefore hurt her entire family. Watching him being warm and charming to her made the hair on the back of my neck stand up.

He smiled and nodded through their exchange, said it was good to see her, and told her he hoped she was staying for dinner.

"Speaking of which, I'm going to head to the kitchen to see what Paulette is making," he said. "Something smells delicious in that direction."

Just before he went to join Mom, his eyes met mine. It was a fraction of a second, but it sent a chill through me.

Nerves and imagination, I told myself.

Nora, meanwhile, whispered that she didn't want to stay for dinner. Dad might be outwardly friendly, but Mom was another matter. You could almost feel the chill coming off her when Nora was there, even though she smiled and spoke politely.

At least Mom was genuine.

"Mom will warm up to you again," I told her, hoping I was right. "It might even help if you were around more. I bet she'd like it if you had dinner with us."

"Maybe if it gave her a chance to poison my food," Nora said.

As she spoke, she intertwined her fingers with mine and leaned close, so our noses were almost touching. She smiled.

It put me off balance for a few seconds and I kind of lost track of what we were talking about. By then she'd moved to a new subject.

"Come on, let's go visit Barnaby. You can make an excuse why I couldn't come back, and I'll meet you later at Jordan's party."

I almost asked who Barnaby was. The only thing that kept me from it was that Nora's body was sooo close, making my brain incapable of forming words. It's also true that with everything going on, Barnaby hasn't exactly been occupying my thoughts on a regular basis. Or any basis at all.

It was a relief when it came to me. Dead rodent. So, instead of asking a question that would have guaranteed a lecture, I scooped her into a sympathetic hug and murmured that it would be really nice to pay our respects to the little guy.

This earned me a shining smile.

We rode our bikes to the cemetery and then walked them through until we reached Barnaby's last resting place.

"Hi Barnaby," Nora said. "We came to see you."

Well, not to "see" you, exactly, I thought.

"I know you and Ethan never got to meet," she said. She gave me a pitying look and patted my arm in sympathy. "But I'm sure you'd have liked each other a lot."

"Definitely," I confirmed.

There was a stretch of silence then, maybe three or four minutes, and I thought she was done, so it startled me when she suddenly let out a sobbing sound and cried, "You were the best guinea pig there ever was, Barnaby!"

I put my arm around her shoulders and pulled her against me.

"I doubt there was ever a guinea pig that was more loved than Barnaby," I said.

Nora hiccupped and whispered, "Thank you for saying that, Ethan."

The weirdest thing happened then. This incredible swell of emotion hit me like a train and the next thing I knew I was — not exactly crying, but something a lot like it. I didn't even know why.

It definitely wasn't, as Nora assumed, about the guinea pig.

For some reason, that changed her mind about coming back to my place to eat. Mom seemed surprised that Nora was joining us, which told me they understood a lot more about each other than I would have guessed.

It went well though. Mom had made two kinds of samosa, served with chutney, a mixed veggie dish of some sort, and saffron rice. Nora said more than once that it was amazing (which it was) and she took seconds of almost everything. I could tell that pleased Mom.

Also, she helped clear the table before we left. Mom likes that sort of thing. She says it shows breeding and good manners.

We stopped by to collect Owen before heading to Jordan's place, which is just two streets over and down half a block. A five-minute walk normally, but Owen was really dragging his feet.

"If this is part of your training routine, you might need to step it up," I said. "It doesn't look like you're about to break a sweat."

He fake-laughed, but made no comeback, which was when I figured out why he was stalling. I don't know why it hadn't occurred to me before then.

There was a good chance Bahiriya Osmani would be at Jordan's party.

Jordan's father only let her have one outdoor bash each summer, but it was guaranteed to be a good one. They had one of the biggest pools in the community and there'd be lifeguards hired for the evening. A live band or top-notch DJ, food stations tended to by guys that we all knew had bouncer duties too, a firepit, and activities that were still fun even though we were a bit old for them.

It always drew a huge crowd. Everyone was welcome as long as there was no trouble. First sign of that and the server/bouncers were right on top of it. It was almost inevitable that there'd be some sort of stir before the night was over, but it was always handled fast.

Being a peaceful type, I liked that nothing was left to get out of hand. I've seen the police called for other parties, but can't remember it ever happening at one of Jordan's.

Anyway, I seem to have wandered off there — I was talking about Owen and what I assumed was his nervousness at the thought of being around Bahiriya. There was no way I could bring up the subject with Nora there though, and no chance to sound him out on anything before we arrived.

And anyway, I don't know what I'd have said if I'd had an opportunity. Besides which, it wasn't likely he'd make any kind of obvious move when there were so many people around. Even if he did, I knew she wouldn't embarrass him on purpose. But that wouldn't stop him from feeling like everyone in a ten-block radius was watching.

By the time we got there he'd developed a full-blown case of jitters. And then, just before he disappeared into the growing crowd, he leaned in and told me why.

"I kind of asked someone to meet me here. She's not sure she can make it though."

He was gone before I could react, and I didn't catch a glimpse of him for nearly an hour. I also didn't see Bahiriya anywhere, but Nora and I were having such a good time I can't say I was paying a whole lot of attention.

It was when we decided to grab a snack that I saw Owen again. The guy in charge of the firepit foods starting flirting with Nora while he speared s'more supplies for her to toast. She giggled and did some hair flipping and posturing that I wasn't appreciating.

"I'm going to take a leak," I told her, hiding my annoyance. "Back in a minute."

It gave me a bit of satisfaction to walk away. I didn't know if she was trying to make me jealous, but if that was her game, I wasn't playing.

When I left the bathroom I took a wander through the crowd, and there was Owen, his eyes glowing and face flushed. I'd have thought he was high if I didn't know one hundred percent that he's full-on anti-drugs.

And there, standing close to his side and smiling up at him, was Kylie — the girl from the gym!

It took me a couple of seconds to get my mouth shut. From the day he'd told me he was interested in Bahiriya, Owen had never mentioned anyone else. Although now that I saw him with Kylie, I remembered him saying, in some passing conversation, that he'd been surprised to find out she was only eighteen.

It was Kylie who happened to look over and see me standing there gawking at them. She lifted her hand in a quick wave, poked Owen, and nodded toward me. They came over.

"You remember Kylie?" he said.

"Sure. She's the mean girl from the gym," I said, grinning.

"That's right," she said. She turned to him to add, "And don't you forget it, Owen."

We talked for a few minutes and then Owen asked me where Nora was.

"She's at the firepit. And actually, I'd better get back to her."

Nora had apparently wrapped up her flirting session and finished her snack, since she was watching a game of pickleball when I found her again.

"How was the s'more?" I asked, sidling up to her.

"So good! You should have had one."

"Maybe later."

It was an excellent night in so many ways.

CHAPTER TWENTY

That party at Jordan's really picked me up. Being able to forget about everything that'd been happening and just enjoy friends, music and good food was awesome. And I slept for eleven hours afterward!

When I got up the next morning, I felt lighter or something. The stuff pressing down on me didn't seem so hopeless. I even found I could let in a bit of optimism. Maybe things weren't as terrible as they seemed.

Just feeling that bit of hope was so great.

Fast forward two days, which is when Dad told me he had a half day at work and I should keep the afternoon open for him. I asked what we were doing.

"You'll see," was all he'd say.

"What does Dad want me for today?" I asked Mom later.

"Ask me no questions and I'll tell you no lies," Mom said. She says that every time she doesn't want to answer something. I've never in my whole life, as far as I can remember, managed to get anything out of her once she says that.

I shrugged and was turning away when she spoke again.

"Oh, Ethan, wait."

"Yeah?"

"Do you have anything for the light laundry? I need a few more things to make a proper load."

I went to look and returned with an armload.

"Why is it that you pile dirty clothes in your room until I ask for them when there's a hamper in the bathroom just a few steps down the hall?

"I'm a bad son," I said. "Where do you want me to put these?"

"In the tall, gray basket in the laundry room."

On my way there I heard her saying behind me, "And you're not a bad son."

It's not often Dad makes plans for the two of us, but when he does it's not unusual for him to keep it secret until the last minute. Even so, I felt a little anxious through the morning. I handled that by going to Owen's house and listening to him talk about how amazing Kylie is. While I was there, I also used his phone to call Aki.

Aki and I had agreed to take a break for a bit after our prowl through the house last week, and to be particularly careful about text messages.

"Hey," I said when he picked up, "it's me. I'm using Owen's phone, just to be safe."

"Good thinking. What's up?"

"Everything seems cool so far. Chances are they don't even know they left the garage door partly open yet. In which case there's no reason for them to have looked at security footage."

"True," he agreed. "And you know what? Maybe they won't even bother. It's not like we left any signs that someone was in there. They might just realize the door stuck and leave it at that."

"Not my father," I said. "He'll definitely insist on checking."

"I guess it won't matter much," Aki said. "Assuming our disguises hid us well enough."

"Except they'll move anything incriminating once they realize someone has been in there snooping around."

We talked for a few more minutes and Aki said to call anytime I needed him back on the job. I almost suggested we should hang out sometime, but I wasn't sure how that would come across. There's no pretending our lives aren't different.

The truth of that really hit me a while later when Dad and I were on our mystery-to-me outing. He'd picked me up right after lunch and made small talk as he drove us to our destination.

A car dealership.

"We're just going to have a look around today," he said. "There are a few places we'll want to check out before we make a decision."

I could barely speak but I managed to say, "Are you serious?"

"It would be a pretty lousy joke if I wasn't," he said, giving my knee a slap.

"But I thought —"

"This wasn't going to happen until after you graduate?"

"Yeah."

"That was the plan all along, but your mom and I have talked it over and we see some good reasons to get you set up with your own car now. For one thing, we'd like you to have a solid year of driving under your belt before you head off to university. We know you haven't had much access to a vehicle since you got your license."

I got my license more than a year ago, but have hardly ever managed to persuade Mom to let me take her car. She pampers that thing even more than she pampers me, which should tell you a lot. And Dad's wheels are registered with his business or something, so the insurance won't cover me.

He shoved his door open and, as he got out, added, "Besides. You're a good kid. We appreciate that."

I was in a daze as we looked over the lot. Dad explained we'd be considering vehicles that were two to five years old with low mileage. I sat in a few, which was ridiculously exciting. Dad got specs from a salesman named Gerry who told us more than once if we had anything specific in mind that we didn't see on the lot, he could certainly put out feelers.

By the time we called it a day, we'd been to four dealerships and Dad had gathered paperwork on nine vehicles.

I was psyched. I pictured myself picking up Nora, free to go wherever and whenever we liked. No more waiting for hired drives, and no more built-in eavesdroppers. I imagined us taking leisurely drives to quaint places where we'd have romantic meals or maybe wander along peaceful, mysterious paths. I had to find such places first, of course, but I was confident they were out there, and that we would build memories that could only strengthen things between us.

After dinner I hightailed it to Owen's place. When he opened the door a glance at his face told me what to expect inside.

Mrs. Cass was smashed.

"Sorry, man," I said quietly. "Want me to go?"

"Nah. It's nothing you haven't seen before. And I could use some company."

I took a few hesitant steps inside, knowing what was coming and cringing at the thought.

"Eeethan! C'mon in!"

She was swaying on her feet, arms held forward, a sloppy smile on her face. There was nothing I could do but go forward and try to give her the briefest hug I could get away with. Unfortunately, brief wasn't possible this time. She got hold of my shoulders and held on — probably more to help her stay upright than anything else. And she leaned in, which is the thing I most dread when she's like this.

"S'good ta seeya, kiddo. Seems like issbeen weeks, hasn it?"

"Uh, it's nice to see you too, Mrs. Cass," I said, trying to lean back without making it too obvious. At this point of intoxication, Owen's mom sends out liberal amounts of boozy spray when she talks. It isn't pleasant.

Owen stepped in as quickly as he could, freed me from the shoulder grip, and eased his mother onto a reclining loveseat. He tugged the footrest out and got her into a comfortable position, all the while speaking to her in a calm and soothing voice. She offered some resistance a couple of time, twisting her shoulders and mumbling something it was probably just as well I couldn't make out.

He and I talked quietly on the other side of the room while she grumbled and muttered and finally nodded off. We gave her a few more minutes before making a quiet exit, with Owen stopping on the way by to tilt her chin down and to the side.

I followed him to the sunroom and got comfortable in a hammock chair. For a change, he didn't wander around fussing over the plants, but sank into the twin of my chair and offered me a grin.

"So," he said. The smile got bigger. "What's up?"

"Seems like something's up with *you*," I observed. "Is it Kylie?"

"It's looking that way," he said.

"That's fantastic," I said.

Owen beamed. Then he told me how he'd started to suspect she might like him and realized he'd lost interest in Bahiriya as he spent time around Kylie. He told me all the good things about her. It was a long list for someone he'd only known a short time.

"So, it worked out perfect," he finished.

I missed the gym connection in that comment, which was okay since he pointed out the pun *and* explained it. That amount of effort deserved a laugh, even if the pun itself didn't. I obliged.

"I have news too," I told him.

"Good news?" he guessed.

"Crazy good — my mom and dad have decided to get me a car now instead of waiting until graduation."

Owen whistled.

"Wow," he said.

"I know, right! Dad took me around to different dealerships today, so we could check out what's available."

"That's — I mean, that's amazing," Owen said. "But —"

He paused then and I think he was trying to decide whether or not to continue. Finally, he did. "Do you think there's any chance it has anything to do with what you just found out?"

"What, about my dad's side hustle? I don't see how."

"Side hustle?" Owen said. He arched an eyebrow.

I felt the heat of embarrassment creep up my neck and face.

"Well, I'm not one hundred percent sure what it is, exactly," I said.

"Since when?" Owen asked. "Since your father bribed you with a car?"

I fought the annoyance that was taking hold before answering.

"It's not a bribe. It was always the plan to get me one — they're just moving it up a bit. And, like I said, this has nothing to do with whatever my dad is involved in."

Owen shrugged. He's the kind of guy who'll tell you what he thinks straight up, but I can't remember him ever pushing his opinion past that. He just kind of leaves you to think it through on your own.

In this case, I wished he was a bit more like Aki, who tried to put a positive spin on things.

Either way, I suppose I knew the truth wasn't going to bend no matter how many theories and opinions there were out there. Except, I wasn't all that eager to dig any deeper, to find out the full extent of whatever that truth was. Not just then.

I'd been looking forward to seeing Nora and telling her about the car when she got off work at nine, but after talking to Owen I decided to wait on that for a day or two.

But boy, I wanted him to be wrong.

CHAPTER TWENTY-ONE

I didn't need Owen to tell me the phrase *side hustle* wasn't the right one for what my father was doing. Somewhere in a part of my brain I was suddenly trying to ignore, I knew very well that my dad was a con man. A criminal, taking money from people who were desperate enough to buy his lies.

Even so, I was as sure as I could convince myself to be that there was no connection between what he was doing and the decision to buy me a car early.

I got this crazy feeling of freedom even in the idea of it. Cruising along, listening to some tunes, stopping anywhere I liked to stretch my legs or check something out.

Mom reminded me the next morning that I might need to be patient.

"You know your father. When it comes to a car, he'll want to check everything twice and weigh all the options until he's sure he's making the best decision."

"I'm getting a say too, though, right?" I said. "He's not just going to go ahead and pick one out without talking it over with me."

"I imagine he'll talk it over with you," Mom said. "But I expect he'll make the final decision. After all, it's a fairly big purchase, and he has the know-how when it comes to these things."

"Right, sure," I said. I knew that was true, and I knew it would be ridiculous to be disappointed if I didn't get to pick out my own car. I wasn't paying for it, and it wasn't like my father was going to get me something that wasn't good.

Telling myself those things didn't seem to make much difference though. It was disappointing to picture myself really, really wanting one car and getting another one instead.

I tried to think of things that might persuade him to seriously consider whatever I preferred, and while I didn't come up with a whole lot, I thought it would be interesting to see how the conversation went.

So, I was pumped when Dad texted me to grab an Uber and come downtown to his office. By the time I got there, everything I'd planned to say had vanished. My heart was beating with the thrill of expectation, and I no longer cared which vehicle it was going to be. All I could picture was my father passing me a set of keys, slapping me on the back, and telling me to drive safely.

The reception desk was, as usual, unattended. I think there used to be someone working it, but Dad decided long ago to use a service instead. So, if you call his office, you get someone working from home, making appointments and so on for clients who no longer need to employ a full-time office worker.

Dad's office door was open and when he saw me, he closed the folder on his desk and waved me in with a smile.

"How's your day going, son?"

"Great. Yours?"

"Actually, that's why I asked you to come down. I need you to look at some images with me and see if you can help me sort something out."

"Okay, sure." He must have narrowed it down and wanted my input on a few top choices.

"Bring that extra chair around here so we can look this over together."

I did that and plunked down, ready to say whatever I could to influence his choice of a car for me.

Then Dad pressed play on a recording and the blood in my veins started to make whooshing sounds in my ears.

This wasn't images of cars. It was video footage from the fake medical clinic, footage featuring me and Aki. I knew instantly that Dad was suspicious, but there was no way he'd be able to tell that I was one of the people in the video. Not with the thrift-store clothes and the headwear all but completely covering my face.

I decided to play it as cool as I could manage.

"What's this?" I said. Because that would be the natural question to ask if I wasn't involved.

"It's a place where another part of my business operates," he said. He was watching the computer screen and didn't even glance in my direction. "Someone has broken in."

"Huh," was all I could manage to say.

"They somehow got in using a keypad entry," he added.

How, in all the scenarios I'd thought about, had I overlooked *that*? Of course he'd know whoever got in had to have had the code for the door lock.

Fighting nausea, I leaned forward as if I was studying the scene. My mouth had gone so dry I didn't know if I could say another word. And then, the intruder in the ball cap — the intruder that was me — made a mistake without even realizing it: he looked up.

Dad tapped his keyboard and froze the image in place.

For a couple of seconds there was an agonizing silence as we both stared at the screen. My face clearly stared back at us.

Finally, when the tension was so tight it felt like something was squeezing my chest, Dad spoke.

"Well?"

I couldn't look at him. And my throat felt like I'd been in the desert for days. I somehow made my legs cooperate enough to get up, cross the room to the corner where a mini fridge sat, and get a bottle of water.

When I returned to the desk I tugged my chair around to the other side, sat down, and forced myself to look at my father.

I don't remember ever feeling so scared in my life. Not even when I was trapped and bleeding in the house my father rescued me from as a child. And yet, in spite of that, something was welling up in me. Not quite anger and not quite defiance. It was a kind of strength born of disgust.

It was also, in part at least, thanks to my dad. I couldn't begin to guess at how many times he's given me advice on how to handle confrontation.

"Never accept the defensive position, son!" he'd say. "Always, immediately, switch to the offensive."

So I did.

"I saw you. When you were supposedly out of town," I said.

He shrugged like that was of no importance whatsoever. But he didn't answer, and I knew why. I knew because of something else he'd told me numerous times.

"The dumbest thing people do when they're under pressure

is talk. You see it all the time in true crime shows. Someone's in the interview room and they think somehow they can explain their way out of a situation."

He'd pause there to laugh — a sound full of scorn.

"A smart person keeps their mouth shut. Because they understand one vital thing, which is this: if they're going to convict you, make them do it without your help."

I don't know how steady I looked, sitting there with my insides in a state of turmoil. But one thing was clear to me. There was no way I could wait him out. He had all the practice, and he had a certain coldness that I was sure I lacked.

All the same, I was determined not to start talking. I knew if I started, I'd keep on and on until he knew everything I'd been up to and what I'd learned.

And *that*, as he'd so diligently taught me, was *not* going to work in my favor.

And so, when I felt the pressure building and sensed I wasn't going to be able to hold out much longer, I took another swallow of water and got to my feet.

"Looks like this conversation is over," I said, wondering at my own nerve.

I started toward the door. Not hesitantly, like I wasn't sure about leaving, but with purpose. To be honest, I'd have loved to get out of there, go somewhere I could be alone and sort things out.

"Ethan," Dad said behind me.

I stopped, but I didn't turn around.

"Sit down, son."

I did as he'd asked, and when I was seated, I forced myself to look him straight in the face. What I saw surprised me. There was something different there, something I'd never seen before. I knew he was rattled, which almost made me feel sorry for him, but the beginnings of sympathy disappeared with his next words.

"Look, Ethan, I'd hate to see you mess up the plans we've just made for you."

Strangely, even with everything else that had happened up until then, when I look back on my life someday, I'm positive that those words, and that moment, are going to form a line marking the before and after.

Because when I heard that statement, when its full meaning hit me, I knew Owen had been right. The plan to buy me a car ahead of schedule was a setup, a pre-emptive strike to keep me in line.

The first flush of emotion that hit me was shame. Strangely, it makes me feel good to say that. Not regret. Not disappointment, but embarrassment at how eager I'd been to be bought. I'm no fool. Even without Owen pointing it out, some part of me had known the truth. I'd refused to face it because I was so busy imagining all the great things having a car was going to do for me.

Right. More like destroy whatever decency and integrity I had.

Then anger came roaring through me like a blast of heat. To be honest, I welcomed it. It drove out whatever nervousness and hesitation I'd been fighting. In a strange way, it calmed me, and let me speak without wavering.

"So, I'm supposed to just act like everything is normal, like you haven't been lying and hiding what you're doing from me and Mom?"

He almost smiled.

"Your mom is a smart woman, son."

"So, you're saying she knows?" I knew, as I asked, that there was nothing he could tell me that would convince me that was true.

"Actually, I'm saying she's aware on some level that things aren't quite as they seem, but she's never asked. Not one time. Which means she'd rather not know."

I didn't believe that either. My mom *is* smart, but there's no way she'd just ignore it if she suspected something fishy was going on.

"Or maybe she trusts you," I said evenly.

Dad ignored that. His eyes narrowed as he spoke.

"The problem here, Ethan, is that you're reaching conclusions without having all the facts."

"So, there are good reasons for what you're doing?"

"Just what is it you think I'm doing?"

This was the place he'd been heading since he texted me to come in. I knew it instinctively, or maybe it was because of all the "tips" he'd given me over the years. I bet he never once thought I'd be using them against him.

My father was digging to find out exactly what I knew, and the only strength on my side was in not telling him. The problem was, I had to give him something — to hold back as much as I could and still confront him.

"There are medical beds in that place," I said after deciding that was the safest approach. One thing I knew was essential was that I didn't give away the fact that I'd found the brochure full of lies and bogus claims. I knew the camera hadn't captured that bit, not only because of the angle in the video we'd been watching but also because if he'd known that, this part of the conversation wouldn't have been taking place.

"And instead of assuming we're doing something good, you jump to the opposite conclusion?"

"If you were doing something good, why would you be hiding it?"

"Who's your friend in the video?" he asked.

Another tactic. Switch subjects suddenly to throw the other person off and possibly make them blurt out an answer. But I was following one of his top rules, which was to always count slowly to three before answering anything. So not only did I avoid the trap, I also went with another one of his tricks and countered with a question of my own.

"Who are *your* friends in this scheme?"

"Look, Ethan, whatever idea you may have gotten, the fact is, we're helping a lot of people."

"Secretly," I said, with no effort to hide my sarcasm.

"Just because something hasn't been approved for use by the medical community, that doesn't mean it's not good."

We went back and forth on that for a bit as I tried, with no success, to pin him down. He wouldn't say anything specific — not about what it was or what it supposedly helped. And he was just as slippery when I questioned the legitimacy of his involvement, considering he had no medical training or background whatsoever.

He spent a couple of minutes talking about how, even if their "alternative method" didn't help everyone, it did something else that mattered.

"It gives them hope," he said. "And hope can have a powerful impact on a person."

"Actual medicine gives them hope too," I answered. "Drugs and treatments that are scientifically proven."

"Not everyone wants to take a conventional path," Dad said.

"Especially if someone persuades them not to."

He shook his head, like he couldn't believe I was being so closed-minded, and we went around the whole thing again. Eventually, I gave up and changed the topic.

"So, if this isn't approved, I'm guessing it could lead to trouble for you, so why do it? Why not avoid the risk and stick to your legitimate business?"

I don't know exactly what it was that I saw in his reaction. A flicker, instantly guarded, a micro-message, like a strobe light of truth, but whatever it was, my response to it was immediate.

How or why I felt so certain of this, I could never explain, but in that moment I knew, absolutely knew, that there *was* no real business.

And as soon as that realization came to me, a lot of things made sense that had always seemed just a little "off" before. The vagueness of his descriptions of what he did. My father is a guy who likes to talk up his accomplishments. The way he'd always answered my questions by disappearing into a maze of words didn't fit at all.

I took a chance and said it.

"There *is* nothing else, is there? This 'medical' thing is your entire business, am I right?"

Naturally, I got no answer to that.

What I did get was a warning, barely disguised.

"We can talk about this some other time, Ethan. You're upset right now, and I can see you need firmer answers. But keep a couple of things in mind for the moment. Besides helping people — which we *are* doing, whether you believe it or not, this venture provides a very comfortable living for our family. If anything happened to disrupt that, it would turn our whole world upside down. Imagine what that would do to your mother."

CHAPTER TWENTY-TWO

I went straight to my quiet place by the Gatineau River. As I sat there, breathing in the blended smells of trees and earth and water, my anger slowly drained away, which would have been good if it hadn't left such a sense of emptiness.

My reality was nothing at all like I'd always believed it to be. As I stared at the truth, I understood that my entire world has been resting on a rotten foundation. I wasn't the son of a smart businessman, living a privileged lifestyle thanks to my father's hard work and wise decisions. There was nothing decent or admirable about my family's standing in the community. It was all a sham, an illusion of respectability.

And what did that make me? The son of a con artist. A kid whose possessions were all bought with money cheated out of sick and desperate people.

Shame filled me, even though none of what my father had done was my fault. Shame, and the feeling that I was a fraud. Someone pretending to belong somewhere I had no business being.

I almost wished Nora and I hadn't patched things up this time. The thought of her embarrassment at learning her boyfriend was the son of a criminal had been bad enough, but knowing her mom was involved complicated things in ways I couldn't begin to predict.

Should I tell her? I knew I couldn't. Somehow, I'd have to act like everything was normal in front of her, right up until the whole scandal became public.

I told all of that to Owen a while later, and when I made the last observation, he raised an eyebrow.

"When the whole scandal comes out?" he said.

"Yeah."

"How's that going to happen?"

I stared at him. As on edge as I was, he looked totally relaxed, slouched in the loveseat of his living room, one leg up over the arm. He shifted a bit and tipped up the energy drink he'd opened a moment earlier. I kept staring as he took a drink and stuck the cap back in place.

"So?" he said.

"I mean, I just thought — it's inevitable, don't you think?"

"How do you figure? If your dad's been doing this for a while, there have to have been complaints. If the police had anything they could get him on, they'd already have shut it down. So, chances are, he'll just keep on his merry way, and nothing will change."

I let that sink in. It was all true.

I'm not proud to admit it, but one of the first things I felt was relief at the thought that life could go on just as it had been. I hated what my father was doing, but I wasn't to blame for it. And in a very few years I'd be out on my own, earning an honest living, being a good person. Who knew, maybe I could even find ways to make up for the wrong my father had done.

But my relief was short-lived. Because Owen wasn't quite finished.

"Unless you do something about it," he said, like he was throwing out an afterthought that had no real importance.

"What can I do if the police can't do anything?" I said.

He shrugged and took a long haul of his energy drink.

"Maybe nothing," he said.

I had a feeling there was more to that comment. I was right.

"On the other hand, it's possible you're exactly what they've needed all along. Someone on the inside who can help them get the evidence they need."

"They could just do that with a search warrant, couldn't they?"

"I don't think so. I mean, I think they have to prove it's justified before a judge will grant a search warrant," Owen said.

"Well, if they had complaints, like you said, wouldn't that be enough?"

"Dude, how would I know? I'm just tossing out ideas. But you know who could answer that question?"

I knew he meant the police, but I had another idea, and it felt like a better choice.

"Let me use your phone for a minute," I said.

"Sure," he said, and passed it over. I had told him weeks ago of my suspicion that my father could be monitoring me through my phone, so there was no need for me to explain why I was asking to use his when mine was right there in my pocket.

Then, because he's genuinely a stand-up guy, he ambled off to the kitchen saying something about getting a snack. I knew his real reason was to give me privacy and I appreciated it.

Making the call only took a minute. I arranged an appointment with Ms. Abboud for the next day and then joined Owen in the kitchen where he was assembling a sandwich of cream cheese with salmon, pickles, raw onion, mayo, and chunky peanut butter. I'm used to his weird food combos, but I hope he never shocks Kylie by slapping something like that together in front of her.

The following afternoon I took the bus and made it to the waiting room of Abboud and Rayne just in time for my appointment. Ms. Abboud's door was shut though, and the privacy blind was closed. I figured she was in there with another client, which proved to be the case when, after a fifteen-minute wait, she emerged from her office, escorted a young couple out, and motioned me in.

"Ethan, it's nice to see you," she said warmly as I took a seat. "I'm sorry about the wait."

"No problem," I said.

"How can I help you today?"

"I need some information," I said. "And advice."

I told her then what I'd discovered about the location she'd found for me. That seemed like a long time ago now, although of course it wasn't really.

She listened without interrupting, jotting a few notes on a yellow pad as I filled her in. I didn't leave out anything except Aki's name. He'd already risked a lot and I wasn't going to be careless and accidentally put him in further jeopardy. I felt I could trust Ms. Abboud but then I didn't know what the law might require if she was ever questioned. Better to say nothing than put either of them in a bad spot.

"My friend thinks there must have been complaints made to the police," I said.

"That's possible," she agreed. "But it may depend on how long this particular fraud has been going on."

"I just assumed he's been doing this for years," I said.

"And that may be the case. But small groups of grifters commonly switch from con to con. It makes it harder to pin them down for any one crime."

It was strange, listening to her talk so matter-of-factly about the whole thing. I appreciated her treating me like an adult, but at the same time I felt like yelling at her to stop. I guess that's the way it's always going to be. How could I get to the place where I'd see my dad as a criminal without some part of me wanting to dispute it?

"This guy who helped me," I said, "he has the brochure and a bunch of license plate numbers from people we assume were getting the so-called treatment."

"You don't have copies?"

"I have a copy of the brochure, but I thought only the original would be useful."

"Useful to the police?"

"I guess. But if there *have* been complaints, and they've already looked into it, there's not much point in me going to them, is there?"

"It's hard to say. I would think the amount of information you could offer them may make a difference. But then, it may not."

"Would it be enough for them to get a search warrant?"

"I would think so. Probably for the location and your house."

"And his office downtown?"

"That's also possible, yes. Wherever he could have records showing any kind of criminal activity. Or evidence that could be related to the scam. Probably what they most need would be proof of him laundering the proceeds. That's likely what the downtown office is used for."

"So, if they got warrants, and found enough to shut everything down and charge my dad and the others," I said, "that's pretty much going to ruin my mom's life."

"And yours?"

"And mine," I agreed, although I didn't like having to say that. "But I graduate next June, and I can make my own choices about what's ahead for me. It wouldn't be that easy for her."

"Don't forget that your life includes your mother," Ms. Abboud pointed out. "Your father too, for that matter. Don't imagine you can really leave this all behind."

"I don't know what to do."

"You're in a tough spot," she said. Her voice was kind.

"I guess I could just do nothing," I said.

"I believe, when you think it through, Ethan, you'll see that doing nothing is also doing something. Whatever choice you make, it's a choice that's going to carry repercussions for someone."

I knew she was right. And that anything she'd told me was based on solid information. But it struck me there was something she didn't know, and I decided it might be worth sharing.

"When I was a little kid," I said, "My dad saved my life."

That might have startled her, coming out of nowhere that way, but her only reaction was a slight lift of her right eyebrow.

"I'm sure there are many reasons for you to feel loyalty — and love, toward your father," she said.

"There are," I agreed, surprised at how completely she'd understood me.

"I wish I could give you the answer you need — tell you what you should do," she said. "But I can't. This is something you need to weigh and consider. And unfortunately, in the end, I don't believe you're going to find a solution you'll be able to feel entirely good about."

I stood and reached into my pocket.

"Thanks for seeing me and talking it over," I said. I extracted my wallet and opened it.

"There's no charge for today," Ms. Abboud said before I could ask what I owed. "This was basically a follow-up consult. It would be included in what you paid previously."

I didn't argue. A lot of my shoebox savings had been used up and while I was far from broke, the expectation that there'd always be more coming was by no means certain.

She walked me to the outer door and wished me good luck. I thanked her again and headed to the bus stop.

I was heading home. Where else could I go?

CHAPTER TWENTY-THREE

I started wondering over the next few days if I might be having some kind of mental breakdown.

The thought didn't come out of the blue. It was due to a sudden eruption of urges I was having. Serious, almost overpowering urges. There were times when I had to get away from everyone and everything because I was sure I'd lose the battle and give in to one, or *more*, of them any minute.

If there's any kind of violent streak in me, I've never been aware of it. I'm the kind of guy who likes peace. I always try to help smooth things over with other people when I can. So, it was unsettling to say the least to find myself feeling the urge to punch my father. Not a cuff on the arm either. I'm talking about seriously hauling off and driving my fist into his gut. Or face.

It felt so foreign to be having those kinds of thoughts. Hit my father? Or hit anybody for that matter, but my own dad? Unheard of.

It wasn't even happening when I was mad either. It might make some kind of sense if we were in an argument, getting more and more furious, but there was none of that. Not only is that not *my* style, it's not his either. I've rarely so much as heard my dad raise his voice. Sometimes it's almost scary how calm he is, even in the middle of a crisis or disagreement.

Mom has always claimed I take after him in that way, which makes what's been happening kind of terrifying.

We'll be at the table, having a meal, maybe having a conversation about nothing important — and the next thing I know, I'm imagining what it would be like to stand up, take a step or two to his end of the table, and just clock him. And then I'm horrified for thinking something like that, but that doesn't stop it from happening again.

Those aren't the only urges I've been getting — just the most twisted. There are also moments when I want to get in his face and scream horrible things. Not just accusations either. That would mean he could be innocent, wouldn't it? No, I want to yell facts about what a lowlife he is until he cringes and slinks away. Assuming he's not a complete sociopath who's incapable of feeling shame or remorse.

There are other impulses but those are the two that are happening the most. And it worries me a little that the moment could come when I'll act on one of them. Which would be devastating, not because he doesn't deserve it, but because that would shove the whole ugly mess out into the open.

Where my mother will see it.

Besides imagining saying and doing awful things to my father, I've been tortured by mental images of how it would affect my mom to find out about this.

When I talked with Ms. Abboud, I got the impression she thought I was using my mom as an excuse, but I honestly wasn't.

The thought of Mom finding out her husband is a con man and her whole life is supported by cheating people who are sick and suffering makes my stomach hurt. I feel sure it would destroy her. It would definitely break her heart.

And yeah, I care about what happens to me too. I'm not an idiot — I know my whole life could be turned upside down. But I could handle it. Mom, I'm not so sure.

And then there's my father. Yes, he's the bad guy in this rotten business. I'm not going to pretend there's anything to defend about what he's doing. There isn't. On the other hand, he's been a decent father to me. It wouldn't even surprise me if he sees me as a big part of his motivation in all of this. He's given me so much over the years. He encourages me and looks out for me.

He saved my life.

It would be so much easier if he was an out-and-out monster. If he was a lousy father. If I didn't love him.

It's been strange and unsettling to discover it's possible to both love and loathe someone.

For days, this upheaval of thoughts and feelings has left me off balance, distracted, and in a constant state of turmoil.

I've started to worry that I might be having some sort of mental breakdown.

Nora didn't help, which wasn't her fault at all. Since I hadn't confided in her, since I had, in fact, done the opposite of that and kept everything from her, she had no reason to see my lack of focus, my rising and falling moods, as anything but odd.

"I might as well not even be here," she told me one afternoon, out by the pool in our backyard.

I pulled my attention back from wherever it had gone at that moment. Gave her a questioning look, and said, "Hey, is that a new swimsuit? Looks great."

"No, it is *not* new and don't try to change the subject. You've been distracted all day. I'm practically sitting here alone."

"Don't you think you're exaggerating just a bit?" I said.

Nora's eyes narrowed and fixed on me. She really hates being accused of exaggeration.

"No, I do not," she said in coldly clipped words.

I figured she'd be breaking up with me any minute. After all, she'd done that over things she only imagined, which wasn't the case that day. I'd paid her next to no attention since she'd arrived. Not intentionally; I just couldn't concentrate. My brain was in some sort of lockdown, circling the same things over and over, unable to break free.

So, I waited for her to tell me that was *it* and we were *done*. It was a surprise then, when she stood, took a couple of steps to the pool, sat on the edge, and lowered herself into the water. She swam to the other end and back a few times, pausing twice to flick water in my direction.

When she got out, wrapped a towel around her waist, and returned to her lounger, she stuck her sunglasses back on and stretched out, her wet skin glistening under the sun. I thought I might be getting the silent treatment, but after a few minutes she spoke.

"You've been different lately," she said. "Since you got hit by the car."

"Different how?"

"It's hard to describe," she said. "It's as if something is missing. Like you're not completely you anymore."

That was the moment I could, and maybe *should* have told her what was happening with my dad. I'd have left her mom out of it of course. For all the times I'd gone over it in my head I'd never thought of a single way I could tell her that without it causing situations I couldn't control.

But I knew, if I told her anything, I'd have had to start with a confession. Admitting I'd been lying to her for more than a month isn't the kind of thing that goes over big with Nora.

All of this — the violent thoughts, the inability to function normally, made me realize that I probably needed to talk to someone. For a few seconds I thought maybe I could make an appointment and go back to Ms. Abboud again. She's so easy to talk to, but I knew that would seem strange.

I know I could discuss it with Owen, or even with Aki. Funny how they're more or less opposites. Owen with his no-nonsense, just-the-facts approach, while Aki looks for the softer, kinder side of things. And then it occurred to me.

"Or both!"

"What?" Nora sat up and peered at me over her shades.

"I uh, was just thinking out loud." But was I? Watching what I say around Nora is pretty much second nature by now. Blurting something out that carelessly was something I'd never done.

First the accusation of overreacting, and now this. It was as if someone else was in control. Someone who wanted to make trouble for me. And meanwhile, Nora was pressing for an answer.

"Thinking out loud about what?"

"It's nothing to do with you."

"So, who'd you mean by 'both'? You definitely said 'both.'"

"Would you just drop it, please?"

"No! I want an answer, Ethan. You can't just say random things and then refuse to explain yourself."

"Apparently, I can," I said. And I smirked at her like someone insane had taken over my face.

She stood up, grabbed her top and shorts from the bag she carries all her swimming and tanning stuff in, and tossed them on over her wet swimsuit.

Here it comes, I thought with an odd feeling of detachment. *Breakup number who-knows-how-many.*

But I was wrong. She gathered her things without speaking, sighed, and said, "Look, I'm going home. Text me when you're done being weird."

I watched her leave, toying with the idea of asking her to stay, saying something to smooth over the way I'd been acting, but in the end, I just sat there staring until she was out of sight.

Then I took a long, slow swim and thought some more about the idea of asking Owen and Aki if we could all meet. Soon. As in, before I cracked up.

It felt like my best option. I made up my mind to do it. So, after the exchange of a few quick messages, we were on for eight that evening. There was a bonus too: Aki had plans with Jean-Guy a bit later, so he asked if it would be okay to bring him along.

"Absolutely," I said, wishing I'd thought to include him without being asked. I didn't know Jean-Guy well, but all of my impressions about him had been positive.

CHAPTER TWENTY-FOUR

We obviously couldn't meet at my place, but Owen, with a quick caution that his mom *might* be around (translation: drunk and bothersome) said we were welcome to come to his house.

I got there half an hour early so I could get a sense of the situation, and therefore the likelihood of a problem. Luckily, his mom was on the couch, leaning on Phil and watching something on TV. She looked drowsy and happy, both hopeful signs that she wouldn't suddenly burst in on us guys with a long and sloppy speech.

Owen told me he'd mentioned to Phil that a couple of other guys were coming over, which was also reassuring. Phil does what he can to keep things smooth if there's a chance Owen will be embarrassed, which was my main worry too.

I know it's tough for Owen, and the reason I'm one of the few friends who's at his place on a regular basis.

But this night turned out all right as far as Mrs. Cass was concerned. Aki and Jean-Guy arrived and after introductions we went out into Owen's sunroom.

Jean-Guy stopped just inside the door and took a good look around.

"Wow!" he said. "Who did all this?"

"You mean the plants?" Owen said, although there wasn't anything else Jean-Guy could have meant. "I kind of mess around with them."

"This is fantastic," Jean-Guy said. "Isn't it, babe?"

"Uh, sure," Aki agreed. He made an effort to look interested.

The next ten minutes or so was spent with Owen and Jean-Guy discussing the different plants. Aki and I found other things to talk about while that went on, and then I got my chance to explain why I'd wanted to meet.

I wanted to be sure everyone had all the details, so I took the time to go over it quickly. The medical scam. The "bribe" of a car. The recent conversation I'd had with Ms. Abboud. The fact that Nora's mom appeared to have some involvement. My certainty that my mother was one hundred percent in the dark.

And then the part that was new, and hard to admit. Thoughts of striking out, either physically or with words. The rage that seemed to be simmering just below the surface. My fear that it would overpower me, and I'd say or do something catastrophic.

"If you can," I said when I'd finished saying everything I wanted to, "try to pretend you don't know anybody involved. Like it's a hypothetical situation about someone else."

"Okay," Owen said. "So, how can we help?"

"Talk it through. Tell me what you think," I said.

"As in, should you take action or not?" Owen asked.

"Basically," I said. "It's haunting me nonstop. What should I do? Should I even do anything at all?"

"Do you want to start with your own thoughts on any of that?" Aki asked me.

"No. I just want to hear what you guys have to say."

The first and biggest thing that came out was whether or not I should contact the police. Jean-Guy suggested making lists of *Report* and *Don't Report* reasons for going to the authorities. We all agreed that was a good idea.

Oddly, it was almost relaxing, sitting back and letting the three of them talk. I liked the way they discussed it, going back and forth on different points.

The list on the *Report* side of the debate was all about victims and the different ways it would be helping them. Except, everyone agreed there wasn't much that could be done for anyone who'd already been conned, so that would mostly help future victims.

Owen said if the fake medical clinic got shut down, people would go ahead and get traditional treatments.

"And they wouldn't be passing over who-knows-how-much money for the privilege of being conned," he added.

"Maybe that's true," Aki said. "But I'm not so sure. After all, these people must be looking for options, or at least open to the idea of alternative treatments."

"They might just find another scam," Jean-Guy added. "Maybe even one that's worse. And they could still get ripped off."

I couldn't help thinking that was like a drug dealer saying if they weren't selling dope, users would just get it from someone else. As if it was okay to commit a crime because other lowlifes were doing it too. But I kept my resolve and said nothing.

After that they moved on to reasons against reporting it and the focus swung around to how that would affect me, my family, and my world.

"Well, here are the results," Jean-Guy said when they'd finished. He passed me the lists and I was shocked at how long the

Don't Report list was. There were at least three times more items on it, as compared to the *Report* list.

Jean-Guy had kept track of it all in point form and even though I'd been there while they talked it over, my stomach clenched reading through the two columns. Not everything on either side was definitely going to happen, but I didn't see anything that wasn't at least possible. The list of reasons *not* to report my dad were pretty much all about me and my family. It started off with this:

- hurt mom
- might destroy relationship with dad forever
- dad could go to prison
- dad could have a criminal record
- dad would not be employable, esp. for good job
- lose their house/vehicles
- have to move
- change schools on graduation year
- lose contact with friends
- massive lifestyle change
- future education plans down the drain
- public humiliation

Those were the main things and it really brought it home to me how massive the consequences of turning my dad in would be. It was world upside down stuff.

I thanked the guys for helping me sort it all out the way they had.

"So," Aki said, "is your choice clearer to you now?"

"I'm not sure," I said carefully. "But the list of reasons *not* to report my father is so much longer than the reasons to do it."

That was true. If they were on a balance scale, the *Don't Report* side would have far outweighed the *Report* side. But there was something else that factored into the equation in a much bigger way and that was how it all felt.

One thing I appreciated them mentioning was that my feelings of rage, the urges to strike out, were a separate matter. They all agreed I should see a psychologist or counsellor — someone who could help me sort that out and deal with it properly.

Lying in my bed a few hours later, I went over it all again.

The list of reasons not to go to the authorities was loaded with things that mattered to me personally. That sounds selfish, I realize, but it's also true. Just thinking about possible outcomes made me nauseous.

My mother was a huge concern, but the truth was that this thing could break *both* of us.

And this comes across as horribly callous, but I'm trying to be honest here. Fact is, the side in favor of reporting the crime affected people I didn't know. Of course, I hated the idea that they were being ripped off, but with no personal connection it was difficult to relate very deeply to the wrongs being done to them.

Sure, I'd sat with Aki, watching people go in and out of the fake clinic, but they were nameless faces, there for a moment and gone. I knew nothing about them or what they were going through. And it occurred to me that a good percentage of the "patients" Aki and I had seen were older, with most of their lives behind them. Mine was still ahead.

I went over it all for hours; I even tried to envision having a conversation with my father where I persuaded him to stop what he was doing.

In the end I felt as stuck as I'd been all along. Unsure about what to do. Unprepared to take a step either way.

The new school year was just over a week away. If I could somehow put it all out of my mind, if I could get through twelfth grade, I just might be able to move on into my future and leave the whole thing behind me.

I told myself I was just putting my life in a holding pattern. That once I'd graduated, I could make a decision more easily.

I knew that was a lie. And a cop-out.

And then, just a couple of days later, I had another urge. A much different kind than those I'd been feeling toward my father. It was strange, and to this day I can't explain it, but it was an overwhelming feeling telling me to go somewhere.

I called Aki to see if he was free. He was. Another "chance" happening that could have changed everything if it had been different.

If he'd been busy, if he'd told me we'd have to go another day — well, who knows what the outcome would have been.

But he wasn't busy, and we did go. He picked me up.

"Where are we going?"

"Remember the old couple, the ones we followed that first time?"

"Yeah."

"I want to go there."

"Like, go and talk to them?"

"Maybe. Honestly, I have no plan. Just a feeling."

It didn't take long to get there. Aki parked on the street near the couple's house. A sign on the lawn caught my eye at once.

"Their house is for sale!"

"Well don't jump to any conclusions," Aki said quickly. "Lots of older people sell their homes when it gets to be too much to take care of a place."

That was true, but how could I find out for sure if it was why this couple was selling? I was wondering if I could hire Ms. Abboud to schedule a viewing and see what she could find out when Aki spoke again.

"Look, a car's pulling into the driveway. Let's get out and take a stroll past the place, maybe we'll pick up on something."

We did, moving slowly along the sidewalk. As we neared the edge of the yard, a man got out of the driver's side and walked around to open the passenger door. He reached down, giving his hand to assist someone out, and when that person emerged, we saw that it was the woman, the one from the old couple we'd followed there.

She looked frailer than I remembered, and a surge of anger clutched me. Was this evidence of failing health because of my father?

It was, but not in the way I thought. As we sauntered slowly past, I heard a moan from the old woman, and the young man with her spoke.

"I know, Mom. I know it's hard. But it's the best thing for you."

"I just never thought I'd be the one left behind," came a thin, plaintive voice from the woman. "Or end up as a burden to my children."

"You're not a burden, Mom. Joanne and I are glad to have you come and stay with us."

"But Dawson and I had a plan," she said, and then she broke down crying. "What fools we were, taking that mortgage to pay for a treatment that didn't help one bit."

"You weren't fools," her son said gently, "you were swindled. But there should be a little something left for you when the house sells, and no matter what you'll always have a home with us."

The old woman continued to cry, and he encircled her frail shoulders with his arm and held her against his chest, murmuring that it would be all right.

I'd heard all I could stand by then. Nudging Aki with my arm I swung around and walked back to the car as quickly as I could. My jaw trembled with fury as Aki slid into the driver's seat.

He waited, silent, looking straight ahead while I steadied my breathing and fought to control the churning in my gut.

"What a monster," I said at last. "How could anyone do that to an old couple? So, the old guy died — maybe because he didn't get the right treatment — and his wife is left in a bind because they were scammed."

"I'm so sorry, Ethan," Aki said.

"What if she didn't have a son ready to take her in?" I said. "What about all the other victims who have no one to help them?"

Aki didn't try to answer, but then I wasn't really asking him.

"You know what?" I said, "I want copies of everything you gathered. All the stuff I didn't want to risk taking to my place. The full list of license plate numbers, the brochure, and all the other notes you made."

Aki started the car. He didn't ask me what I wanted it for. He just drove to his place and for the next forty minutes we worked with barely a word between us, copying page after page of information and notes. Then he put all the photos he'd taken whenever he had a clear enough shot to get pictures of people coming out of the "clinic" on a thumb drive.

"These too?" he asked, flicking through the pictures of Nora's mom's car, including the one where her face was easily recognizable. I realized as I scanned them that her license plate was clearly visible in two of the photos.

I hesitated. Then I said, "Yes."

He added them, put the drive and all of the other evidence into a bag, and passed it to me.

"You want a lift?" he asked.

"Please."

When he pulled up to the police station Aki offered to go in with me.

"No. Thanks, but I need to do this by myself. Is it okay if I give them your name and contact information though?"

"Definitely."

And then I was there, on the sidewalk, alone. I watched as he gave a short wave and drove off. I stood for a few minutes after he'd disappeared from sight.

I felt sick. And scared. It took a crazy amount of effort to make myself walk up to the door.

And that's where I stood. Once again frozen in place, feeling the strength of my resolve beginning to waver.

My hand was on the door handle. I remember looking at it like it belonged to someone else. My heart was hammering like mad. My knees threatened to fail me.

I'd made up my mind. I was there to do the right thing. And yet …

I still had a choice.

I glanced up, saw my reflection in the glass. And I knew — the guy staring at me was going to remember what he did at this moment for the rest of his life.

EIGHT MONTHS LATER
CHAPTER TWENTY-FIVE

Looking back on that day, I remember how the door was surprisingly heavy. It took a good hard push before it yielded.

I stepped inside.

The next few hours were a muddle of questions. When it was all over, I went to the washroom and was sick. Then I went home and spent a few weeks in a blur of anxiety, knowing that any day a knock was coming at the door.

It was the third week of school when it happened. Dad was at home, working in his office, when they landed with a search warrant. I found out later they'd hit his downtown office and the fake clinic all at the same time.

Between the evidence they got that day and the witnesses they talked to from the license plate numbers I'd given them, they had more than enough to shut the place down and bring charges.

I don't know if he was tipped off or just lucky, but two days before the detective came with a warrant for his arrest, my father disappeared.

We haven't seen or heard from him since.

At first all I could feel was relief. From the day they did the searches until the day he drove off without a word to either Mom or me, every minute I'd spent around my dad had been torture. The way he looked at me, his jaw set, his eyes dark with anger — I can't even describe what it was like. But maybe cold fury was easier to handle than sadness or heartbreak would have been.

I tried a couple of times to talk to him, to explain that I had to do what I felt was right or to remind him I'd all but begged him to stop. If he'd stopped, I could have let it go, but I knew that was never going to happen. More and more people were going to be hurt, physically, mentally, and financially. And if I did nothing, I knew I had to share in his guilt.

The first month with him gone was like living in one of those nightmares where you're trying to move but you can't. I couldn't think straight. Some days I couldn't make myself go to school, even though it's my last year.

I soon found out, though, that I'd been incredibly wrong about my mom. As in, I'd underestimated her completely. Dad had told her not to worry about anything after the searches were done. He refused to answer her questions, insisting it was all too complicated. At the same time, he reassured her everything was under control, it was all a mistake, and everything would be fine. I think she tried really hard to believe him. Until he left, and then she couldn't. And that was when things changed.

For a few days she seemed to be in a kind of fog, and while I didn't see her cry, her eyes were red and puffy a lot. When she spoke to me it was like someone on autopilot. But by the end of the first week, she was starting to come around, and by the end of the second week she was spending most of her days sorting through documents, bank records, and contracts. She put in a lot of time on the phone, and she made a bunch of appointments to see people.

When she'd had a chance to figure out the basics, she sat me down.

"You're nearly an adult, son, and you've just done a very adult thing. And in case you ever wonder or second-guess yourself, you need to know that you did the right thing. That took a lot of courage. I want you to know how proud I am of you for that."

I couldn't speak.

"There might be — no, there *will* be some tough times ahead, but we *will* be able to handle them, okay?"

Then she gave me the hard facts. The house was in her name, which sounded like great news at first since all of my father's assets had been frozen pending the trial. The problem was, the house had been remortgaged a few times. Mom had never questioned it when Dad got her to sign bank documents; she'd trusted he was making good decisions.

The bottom line on the house was that there was very little equity built up, and an enormous monthly mortgage payment.

There was almost no money. Not that she had access to anyway. So, the house had to be put on the market right away. It sold quickly and the money that was left was just enough for Mom to get a decent secondhand car (her big fancy leased SUV had been returned to the dealer by then) and help us get set up in an apartment. We moved on December first.

The irony was not lost on me that we'd lost our house just like the old woman I'd seen crying to her son. And my father had caused it in both cases.

I thought I'd have to change schools but that didn't happen. That was good in a way, but there have been a lot of days it's been hard to be surrounded by kids who know all about my father. And that I turned him in.

There's no denying some of them treat me differently. Sometimes I hear snide comments about being careful around The Informer and stuff like that. I keep walking. It's gotten less as the months have passed, and now, with graduation just around the corner, it hardly matters anymore.

The thing that was weirdest was the way a few former friends started to look at me as less than I was before. Not because I reported my dad though. Because I'm now what they consider poor.

That feels horrible sometimes, but I kind of pity them too. Nobody knows what tomorrow might bring their way. I sure didn't see any of this coming. But to base your opinion of a person's value on money, or the lack of it — man, that's truly pathetic.

I'll admit right now that sometimes it bothers me, feeling poor. I can't say it doesn't matter, of course it does. It's unfamiliar and it doesn't yet feel natural to live without the advantages I had before. But it's not as awful as I thought it would be. As cliché as this sounds, I've been discovering what really matters.

Owen and Aki and Jean-Guy have been amazing supports. They're always ready to listen or talk or both, and they've helped me a lot on some of the darker days. I spend a lot of time with them, sometimes just one, sometimes all three. In the first few months, both Owen and Aki made sure they connected with me every single day, even if it was just a text.

Most of that was just friends being there, but now and then there'd be a nugget of advice. The one that really hit me was something Aki told me his mom had impressed on him all through the years.

"Bro, we're young and strong and healthy," he said. "There is no amount of money, and nothing you can possess, that could ever buy you even one of these things."

I think about those words a lot. I hope I never forget them, no matter what I achieve in my lifetime.

In the fall I'm starting my bachelor's program. Owen and I are doing our first couple of years online, which takes some of the pressure off as far as knowing what we want to do with our lives later on. And it's what we can afford, even with student loans and part-time jobs. I'm fine with that.

I don't want to lie, so let me admit there are still days when I think about how life was before all of this, and a part of me wishes I could turn back the clock. It's especially hard when I think about Mom, who's working full-time through the week and part-time on the weekend just to keep us going. I hate it when she looks tired and discouraged and almost puzzled, like she can't quite figure out how her life brought her to this place.

And then there was Nora. She amazed me when the arrests were made.

"This is going to make our bond even stronger," she said, "because no one else can ever know what it's like to go through it."

She meant, of course, that her mother being involved created a special kind of understanding between us. And it did.

Because even though she knew by then that I'd gone to the police about my dad, she assumed they'd uncovered her mom's role in the whole thing during their investigation.

I didn't tell her otherwise. What reason would I have for admitting I knew turning in my father was also going to spell trouble for her mom? The outcome was going to be the same either way.

As she'd predicted, we grew closer than ever before. It was like a shining reward, making up in a small way for all the stuff that was dark and awful.

Her mom's part had been pretty much as I'd figured. She'd provided my father and his partners with names and addresses of people who were being treated at the critical care center where she worked. It wasn't the only way they recruited victims but access to people at the most desperate times of their lives was an essential source.

The prosecutor offered her a deal. No jail time — just probation, provided she cooperated fully and testified when the time came. She took it, but she lost her job, of course, and that hit the family hard.

According to Nora, her mom would never have gotten involved if they hadn't needed the extra income. And maybe that's true, but you can always find a way to justify doing the wrong thing, can't you?

Well, it might have raised their income for a while but now they're struggling to stay afloat. Nora's dad has taken a second job, and her mom is working at a shopping center making a whole lot less than she used to at the critical care center. I feel bad for Nora, and her dad, because they did nothing wrong.

Anyway, like I said, the whole thing brought us closer together. Until — I guess it was nearly three months after the arrests — the third weekend in December, when she actually asked.

She was snuggled up at my side and she'd been crying because her mom was depressed, and her dad was hardly around.

"I hate being in the house now," she told me. "It's like living in a funeral home or something. No one is ever happy. We used to do things, have fun, but that's all gone."

"I know," I said, even though our experiences were quite a bit different. But I *did* know what it was like to have life as you know it crumble around you. "It will get better."

"You always tell me that," she said. "And I know you have it worse in lots of ways. It's just hard to see how things are going to get better."

"Try to think about the positives," I said. "At least your mom isn't going to prison."

Nora shuddered and her arms tightened around my waist.

"I can't even imagine that," she said. "And I know that's going to happen to your dad when they find him. That has to bother you."

"Of course it does."

"I could never have done what you did, knowing what it would mean," she said.

I said nothing, and for a moment there was silence. Then Nora leaned away a bit, looked up at my face, and asked the question.

"You had no idea my mom was involved though, right?"

I've wondered if that question just occurred to her then, or if she'd been carrying it around for a while. Doesn't matter now.

It was tempting to pretend I hadn't known anything about her mom. She might never have found out the difference, and things were so good between us at that point.

But I couldn't do it. There had been so many lies, so much deception. I couldn't make the choice to add to that.

"I never knew how to tell you this, but I did suspect your mom might be involved. I just didn't know for sure."

I don't know what I expected. That we'd talk it out maybe? That she'd be upset for a while but come to understand I'd done what I had to do?

Instead, she pulled away from me and was on her feet in an instant. Her face was wild.

"Are you seriously telling me that you knew, and you *did that to me* anyway?"

I didn't answer. It was clear there was no point.

She had a lot more to say before she left. And I knew that was it between us. We haven't spoken since that day, although now and then she sends a text telling me what she thinks of me.

So, yeah. There's been a lot of fallout and I know it's not over yet. But in a really weird way, I'm starting to see some good things coming out of this. It's hard to explain it without sounding kind of vain, but I know for sure I'm a stronger and better person now than I was before this happened.

I think I'll leave it at that.

ACKNOWLEDGEMENTS

I am privileged and grateful to be working with some of the finest people in the publishing industry.

My publisher and editor, Barry Jowett. Probably Barry is getting tired of hearing how much his insights, suggestions, and encouragements matter. Well, sorry for being repetitious, Barry, but you rock.

And honestly, all of the folks at Cormorant/DCB Young Readers are just plain lovely to work with. In particular, I very much appreciate the work done by copyeditor Gillian Rodgerson, as well as the behind-the-scenes efforts of Sarah Cooper, Sarah Jensen, Luckshika Rajaratnam, and Marijke Friesen.

Thank you all.

I also acknowledge, with sincere thanks, the Canada Council for the Arts, whose support made it possible for me to focus on this project.

VALERIE SHERRARD is the author of more than 30 books for children and teens, including the multi-award-nominated *Birdspell* and the novel-in-verse *Standing on Neptune*. Her work has won or been shortlisted for the TD, GG, Geoffrey Bilson, Ann Connor Brimer, and CLA Awards, and numerous readers' choice programs including the Forest of Reading, MYRCA, Red Cedar, RMBA, Willows, and Hackmatack Awards. Born in Moose Jaw, Saskatchewan, she now lives in Miramichi, New Brunswick.

We acknowledge the sacred land on which Cormorant Books operates. It has been a site of human activity for 15,000 years. This land is the territory of the Huron-Wendat and Petun First Nations, the Seneca, and most recently, the Mississaugas of the Credit River. The territory was the subject of the Dish With One Spoon Wampum Belt Covenant, an agreement between the Iroquois Confederacy and Confederacy of the Ojibway and allied nations to peaceably share and steward the resources around the Great Lakes. Today, the meeting place of Toronto is still home to many Indigenous people from across Turtle Island. We are grateful to have the opportunity to work in the community, on this territory.

We are also mindful of broken covenants and the need to strive to make right with all our relations.